Fortune's Mate

By
Robbie Cox

Fortune's Mate
By Robbie Cox

First Edition
copyright @ 2021

Book Cover Graphics & Art: Beautiful Mess Graphics
Book Cover Layout: Beautiful Mess Graphics
Editing by CTS Editing
Formatting by CJC Formatting

www.robbiecox.com

ISBN: 978-1-955049-06-1
Library of Congress Control Number:

PUBLISHING

To Gary and Shannon, for always being there

Acknowledgments

When life goes crazy, you find out who your true friends are. Ezra found that out in *Fortune's Mate*, but over the past couple of months we've discovered the same thing in our own lives. As our family was struck with some news that shook us up quite a bit and forced us to reevaluate somethings, there were people who stepped up to take some of the load from our shoulders. Amy and Tiffany McClendon, the Spell ladies, and so many more. There have been notes of encouragement, texts asking how things are, and prayers and positive thoughts sent out. As I struggled to finish this book, not because of the story, but because of what was happening in our personal lives, these people kept us going forward and showed to us that the people of Bull Creek are everywhere. Family is not by blood, but by a deep love that flows between people. These people are our family, and I thank them for everything they do to prove that to us.

I also need to thank the three ladies who make this life worth living: Charleen Cox, Teri Edney, and Sarah Mick. These are my Destined Mates, and I would be lost in the woods without them. They keep me motivated, encouraged, and sometimes, even dressed. No matter what life throws at us, I know with these precious souls in my life, there is nothing we can't face, no foe we can't defeat, and no disease we can't conquer. These ladies rock!

I also need to thank the other authors of A Scribbler's Retreat on Facebook. It was their encouragement and writing sprints three or four times a day that helped me get the words in on this manuscript and finally finish it on time. If you're an aspiring author or an established one, I encourage you to find this group and join. You won't be disappointed.

Chapter One

Winifred Preston, or Winnie as she preferred to be called, stretched out along the bank of Crabgrass Creek, her bare feet pointed toward the water as she leaned back, holding herself up by her palms, and allowed the sun to bathe her face. A light breeze blew off the creek, caressing Winnie's skin as she closed her eyes and soaked it all in, allowing the energy of the elements to recharge her batteries. It was time to unwind and relax, bask in Mother Nature's beauty. Opening her eyes, she glanced around at the oaks and cypress, the towering pines and palm shrubs. Bull Creek was beautiful, that was for sure. And peaceful. She was surprised other witches hadn't swooped down on the small community and made it their own yet. Of course, she was glad, as well. It meant she had the place pretty much to herself for now, and she needed the solitude at the moment. Besides, visiting this area was one thing; living there day in and day out quite another. She would enjoy the isolation while she could, however, before returning to the bigger city. A shuffling of feet behind her, though, told her she only had so much quietness available to her, and even that was about to be shattered.

Sitting up, her legs still stretched out in front of her, she glided her hand over the tall grass, reaching out for the elements around her. Closing her eyes once more, she took a slow breath in, feeling the energy of the soil beneath her, the water in front of her, the air surrounding her. *Dear Goddess, thank you for these gifts.* She slid her fingers under the soil, covering her hand with the coolness of the dirt, and reaching out to the roots of the nearby trees with her senses. *I'm not here to hurt you, my dears. Just to explore your history. Show me what has transpired in this part of your universe.* She could feel the darkness that had filled Bull Creek recently, the fights among alphas, the betrayal of family, the threat of outsiders. She saw a woman kidnapped by shifters, used as a pawn to lead the community's alpha to them in order to kill him. Then a scene played out of a father attempting to kill his son and sending his mate off to be sold on the black market. From there, a special forces group rescued a small girl and kept her from being kidnapped by an evil man. Yet, she could also feel the strength of the community's residents, their resolve to protect the people they lived with, celebrated with, and fought with. They defeated the man who attempted to steal back his girlfriend and abuse her again, and they stood tall against a group called The Order of Wardens, who wanted nothing more than to wipe the paranormals from the face of the earth. She saw every battle, and she saw them win every time. They had survived, but more than that, they had thrived, coming together and experiencing life together, not just as like-minded paranormals, but as a family.

Opening her eyes, she slid her fingers out of the soil, wiping the dirt from her hands. Yes, Bull Creek had it all, everything she needed to begin again. Now, she just needed to figure out where to set up shop if she was going to tell these people their fortunes and guide them down the path they needed the people of this small community to follow, whatever that was.

"Well?" the deep voice came from behind her. "Did your little trick work?"

She didn't turn around, but instead kept her gaze fixed on the creek in front of her, trying her best to maintain her grip on the peacefulness of her surroundings. She didn't need to look behind her to know that Deran Sheridan towered over her with his six-foot-four frame, his thick arms crossed over his chest, the breeze tousling his short-cropped dark hair while he glared down at her over his narrow, beak-like nose with his judgmental brown eyes. His impatience loomed over her like a dark cloud. His power was stronger than hers, which is why she catered to him so often, but he also possessed a darker streak than she did when conning people. He held no conscience when it came to separating honest people from their cash or whatever else he wanted from them. It's what had caused them to wind up there in the first place, having been run out of one town after another, escaping a place just before the law or some other less than desirable group got their hands on them. She liked what she had found in the elements surrounding Bull Creek, though. She didn't want to be run out of this town because of Deran and his schemes. As strange as it was to admit to herself, and she would never admit it to Deran for fear of him simply laughing at her, from what she felt in the ground, she could see herself living here permanently.

She felt family here, and none of them were related, their bond forged by something deeper, much deeper.

"There are good people here," she told him, knowing he expected a full report of her findings, but also knowing he probably wouldn't like what she told him. "They've faced some hardships but overcame each one of them. They're a determined people, close-knit and loyal to each other. You may have a hard time getting past their defenses, though, and finding out the information you need. They've seen enough to make them skeptical of anyone new. You may want to tread slowly, if you tread at all."

Deran scoffed. "As if we have time to tread slowly, and we have no choice but to move forward." He shook his head as he glanced around at the nearby trees. "Do you detect any other witches in the area?"

She nodded, tilting her head to the side a little as she reached back down to the soil, closing her eyes as her senses stretched for the roots of the nearby trees once more. *Just me again, my friend. No harm to you, I promise. I just want to learn what you can teach me.* "There is residue of magic being spent. Not much, which tells me one witch lives here, maybe two at most. The rest were run off more than a year ago from what I can gather. Protective wards surround the place, but their power is fading, almost gone."

"She doesn't keep up with her magic?" he asked, his tone one of disbelief. "Not very smart of her."

"Their enemies came in another guise," she answered him, still searching the memories of the trees. "Family. Friends. Humans. A different enemy each time, it seems." She opened her eyes, turning now to face him as she pulled her hands from the soil. "She wouldn't be able to predict each new threat. I think these wards were for something specific, or perhaps someone specific, that no longer poses a threat to them." She stood, running her hands along her backside to knock away the dirt. Turning, she stared at Deran, wishing she could deter him from his current course. "Are you sure you want to do this? From what I could gather, these people have been through enough."

He cocked his brow at her, his lips twisted in a smirk as he placed his hands on his hips. "Are you developing a conscience for our marks now? That's unusual of you."

She made a slight shrug, trying to appear as if it didn't really matter to her. "We usually go after people who deserve it, the lowlifes and criminals. People with enough to spare or something to atone for. From everything I can read from the roots of the trees, these people deserve to be left alone, not taken advantage of. We're the biggest criminals in the area." She sighed, the truth of her statement penetrating her conscience. "Why are we even here in the first place? This is a small haven, a backwoods town that offers mosquitoes and alligators and very little else. These paranormals have made it their safe haven for the disenfranchised and disillusioned. We should honor that, being paranormal ourselves. What's here that you want that we can't find somewhere else?"

"Are you kidding? You felt the power in the soil just now." He gestured to the creek. "Water flows in all directions, small pockets of lakes and ponds dot the landscape, trees that have survived the logging industry here for years. It's a perfect location between the major city to the west and the beaches to the east. Backwoods? Winifred, this is prime real estate. Bull Creek could be the perfect place for us to set up a major coven here in complete secrecy and still manage to have everything we need. And it's already chock full of sacrifices for the blood magic we need to perform."

She stared at him, choosing to say nothing about his use of the word sacrifices. "You need witches for a coven," she said, instead, wondering when his plans had grown to such elaborate proportions. "Where exactly do you intend on getting those? You think people will actually want to leave their homes to come out to this dismal location? There's nothing here except a cheap diner, a bar that caters to the paranormal around here, and a rundown gas station. Even the sheriff's department runs with a minimum force. I mean, it's beautiful, don't get me wrong, but it's also kind of isolated. You're talking forty minutes in either direction before you reach an honest to god town. They'll go crazy with boredom. What do you think this place has to offer those you want to bring here? Because, to be honest, I don't see it." She saw it for herself, but not for others. She had simple tastes, but those witches used to big city life would never survive the isolation of the place.

His grin grew as he stared at her, and his eyes held that same twinkle in them that always warned her when he was about to drag them into one of his nightmare schemes. "A chance to practice their blood magic, of course, to tap into the darkness within them, and bring it to bear. This is where we'll start our mission to subjugate the other races, to make all paranormals, and even the humans, bow down to us."

"You couldn't be happy just taking their money, huh?" She crossed her arms over her chest as she shook her head, sighing. "Deran, your vision of ruling anything is not realistic. I'm telling you, these people have already defeated anyone who's tried to drive them out of here. They're a tougher lot than you're giving them credit for. Why ask for my information if you don't intend to use it?"

He turned, dropping his arms to his sides as he walked off toward the dirt road and their car. "I do intend to use it, Winifred. It's going to show me how to defeat these people where no one else has succeeded. I'll use their mistakes to sharpen my knowledge." He stopped, turning to look at her once more, narrowing his eyes at her. "And you'll be there to help me do it, my distraction for when I steal their town. Don't forget your place." He turned back around, his glare shifting into a false smile. "Besides, it was promised to me. Now, come on. I have you a cabin in this quaint little community. We need to get you settled, so we can both begin our information gathering. You know who will be here in a couple of days, and you know how he hates waiting."

"You know who? I thought we were doing this on our own. Who's coming here? You didn't tell me someone else was—" And then it all fell into place. "Wait a minute," Winnie called after him, rushing to catch up. "This isn't your plan, but his? Mattox is coming here? Why?" Everything just took a spin for the deadly.

Deran grinned at her as he stopped and turned once more to face her. "Because, my dear Winifred, besides the location and resources, Bull Creek possesses one key thing that Mattox craves above all else."

"What on earth could this place possess that Mattox could possibly want? There's literally nothing of true value here. I just got through telling you that." Why had she not asked about Deran's motives before agreeing to this? If she had known Mattox Rumfield was behind this, she never would have agreed to any of it. The man left bodies in his wake wherever he went. "What does Mattox want from here?"

Another smirk twisted Deran's lips as he stared at her, obviously pleased that he knew something she didn't. God, there were times she just wanted to zap that smug expression off his face. With a bounce of his brows, he simply said, "Why, the man who killed his brother, of course."

Chapter Two

A nother beer?" Wes Stapleton asked as he stared across the bar at Ezra. "You know, if you're going to use my bar as an office, you could at least purchase more booze. Otherwise, Jake may want to start charging you rent."

Ezra glanced up from his laptop, a confused furrow on his brow as he heard the other man laughing. "Charge me rent? For what?" He closed his eyes and took a deep breath, nodding as a low, deep chuckle slipped past his lips. "I get it now," he said, opening his eyes. "Sorry. Sitting here is better than working from home by myself. And yes, I'll have another beer. Thanks."

Wes pointed to the laptop as he walked over to the beer cooler under the bar. "What exactly are you working on, anyway, if you don't mind me asking?"

Ezra shrugged as he leaned back on his stool. "I'm helping Julian out," he said as he stretched his stiff muscles. He hadn't realized how long he had been bent over his laptop. "He needed some research done, and the rest of the team is out on a mission. I had some time on my hands and could use the work, so he hired me on contract. It helps break the monotony."

"Julian? He's that vampire that leads your old group, right? Para-Force or something like that?" Wes nodded as he set another beer in front of Ezra and then leaned on the bar. "It hasn't been that long since the whole town helped save that little girl." He cocked his head, narrowing his eyes as he looked over at Ezra, his brows pinched in question. "Did they ever tell you how she's doing? The girl that is."

Ezra nodded, remembering the period Wes brought up. It had happened just over a year ago when his old team appeared asking for his help. At the time, Ezra was living in a tent in the woods, hiding from the world. The fact that his old team even knew where he hid back then had surprised him, but in the end, he couldn't walk away from their need. Not that Josh Rayburn would permit him, too, anyway. Soon, they were confronting one of his old nemeses, Hoyt Cheffron, who had killed a girl Ezra was supposed to protect and then turned around and kidnapped another one. Ezra helped them ensure the girl's safety and, in the process, found a home among the residents of Bull Creek. "Julian put Erin in a school that would help her control her abilities. From what I hear, she's doing fine. Quite powerful, too." Erin Fletcher had only been ten at the time Liam Lamont and Colton Stokes appeared at Ezra's campsite with her in tow. Just looking at that little girl then brought back all the anguish Ezra felt at the other girl's death. However, it was also the kick in the ass he needed to get over his self-pity and get on with his life. Even at such a young age, Erin possessed amazing powers, able to throw pieces of herself into other objects, able to see and hear whatever was happening. At the time, a part of her essence had infiltrated her favorite doll, which also helped them save her.

Wes chuckled as he leaned on the bar. "I remember her. She had some major power back then for someone so small. I'm glad they're able to help her control it. Who knows what would have happened if the wrong person had gotten his grubby mitts on her?"

"Truth," Ezra said, reaching for his beer and lifting it in a toast. After he took a long swallow, he set the bottle back on the bar and returned his attention to his work, and Wes moved to the other end of the bar to serve a couple who had just wandered into Everglades. The sound of two pool balls striking each other ripped the quietness of the bar, causing Ezra to turn and glance at the new back edition to the paranormal bar, still surprised at how much the place had changed. A few months ago, members of The Order of Wardens, an anti-paranormal group, had practically demolished the place, spray painting vile messages on the walls, tearing up the inside, shattering bottles of booze. The broken-down jukebox was about the only thing they couldn't destroy, not that they hadn't tried, of course. The place was almost unrecognizable. However, Jake Goodman, now mated to Noel Hastings and Wes, had stepped up, pitching into the business and offering to help them rebuild. Since they had to do some major repairs anyway, Jake also recommended some changes as they went, such as the two new pool tables in the back and a few dartboards. So, the resident triad of Bull Creek, expanded the building and added more things to entertain the locals. So far, it seemed to be paying off fairly well.

Ezra turned back around, glancing at his screen once more as he scanned over his research. Bull Creek had seen its fair share of nightmares over the past year and a half, from when Para-Force brought that sweet, little girl there in order to keep her safe to fighting gang members who came there to kill a special witness to Dimitri's father trying to kill his son's old girlfriend. The chaos never seemed to end, which seemed to be what made him accept Julian's request when it came through. Ezra missed the action, being part of a team like Para-Force, the adrenaline that rushed through him when out on a mission, and there were always plenty of missions, always another bad guy who needed taken down to protect the innocent.

He scrolled through some of the notes he took for Julian, wondering how far into the Dark Underworld the team would go this time to root out the bad guy. He shook his head, thinking again of how there always seemed to be a new villain somewhere making everyone else's life miserable. Or trying to, anyway. Why people couldn't be happy playing Frisbee Golf or going to concerts and drinking over-priced beer was beyond him. They always had to be stirring up shit. Right now, the team was searching for a group calling themselves The Iron Dagger, who seemed to be intent on hunting shifters for their coats, stripping them while they were alive. Ezra wasn't sure how they kept the shifters from transforming when they started to shed their coats, nor was Julian, which is why he asked Ezra to dig into it. The task wasn't exactly the adrenaline rush of his assignments of old, but it kept him in touch with the others, something he hadn't realized he missed until Julian had reached out.

As he was reading through the notes, a message popped up on his screen from Tyra Pellington, the team's computer whiz. *Hey, you; it's been a long time since I've seen this name on here. I missed it. How's the research going?*

He felt the smile crease his face as he pictured the fiery redhead sitting at her desk, pounding away at her keyboard. She was a scrappy woman with alabaster skin, but she was always there when the team went deep into any mission, most times pulling their asses out of the fire just before they found themselves scorched. *I'm still not sure what Julian expects me to find that Benny can't discover with his Underworld connections, but I'm enjoying the work. How are things there?*

Benny Hastings was a coyote shifter with a dark past, which is why Julian had hired him. Most of the team still had issues trusting Benny, but Julian always counted on the information the oily-looking man could bring to the table.

That's why I'm reaching out actually.

What? You didn't reach out because of my charming personality? he typed back to her, chuckling as he punched the keyboard. *My wounded pride. I may not recover.*

Please, outside of Colton, you have the thickest hide of us all. No, what I wanted to warn you about is that Mattox Rumfield has surfaced again. We're not sure where he's at or even where he's been since we last had eyes on him, but I thought you should be given a heads up, anyway. He wasn't exactly pleased the last time we had a run-in with him.

Ezra nodded, his lips pressed tightly together. Pleased was definitely not the term to describe Mattox's attitude, not when his brother's crimes brought about his death. Mattox swore vengeance then against the team, Ezra specifically for being the one to bring his brother down. Ezra never really worried about it, though. Everyone on Para-Force had enemies. It was part of doing their job and putting the criminals away. He shuddered to think how long the list was of people who would love to have his head on a spike. Besides, he highly doubted Mattox could find him all the way out in Bull Creek. It wasn't like Ezra was easy to find, and Bull Creek was a haven for those who had nowhere else to go, so they were pretty well hidden and protected. Of course, that hadn't kept Hoyt Cheffron from finding little Erin Fletcher a year ago.

Thanks for letting me know, he typed back. *I'll keep an eye out, although I would be hard-pressed to say he could find me way out here.*

Really? We found you. Don't forget that.

He chuckled as he read her words. He took another swallow of his beer before he typed back. *Well, he's definitely not you, and unless you're working for Mattox, I think I'm safe. No way that man has your skills.*

True, but just in case, watch your ass. I'd hate to see anything happen to you.

Thanks. I appreciate it. I'll be careful.

You better be, or I'll make a special trip down there myself. Now, get back to your research. Julian's eager to see what you come up with.

He nodded, smiling. *Tell him, I'll reach out as soon as I have something. Take care.* Reaching for his bottle, he took another long swig, the cold liquid refreshing as it filled him. So, Mattox had surfaced again. Ezra wondered what had brought him out of his hole. He assumed the man would have remained hidden forever after their last encounter, barely having escaped with his life as it was. Something had to have either spooked him to make him resurface or intrigued him enough to make him take the risk.

Ezra shook his head, scrolling through the notes a little more, forcing himself to focus. It didn't matter what had brought Mattox to the surface; he was a file from the past and nothing to do with the present. However, The Iron Dagger was very much the present, and Ezra needed to find something out about them before more shifters were killed. Shoving Mattox out of his mind, he focused on the screen in front of him, looking for any nugget that would help Julian and the others, thinking how sick some people had to be to want to hang a person's skin on their wall. The fact that someone had come up with a way to freeze a shifter's transformation once they died said how perverted the minds of some people were.

"Have you thought about just joining them again?" Wes asked as he slid back in front of Ezra on the other side of the bar.

"Para-Force?" Ezra shook his head. "Not really." He chuckled, shrugging. "Seems, at times, Bull Creek has enough action to keep me on my toes and filling all the needs for excitement I have."

Wes pointed at the laptop. "And yet, you're sitting here, working for them. Seems you miss it at least a little, and you don't strike me as the analyst type."

Ezra glanced down at his laptop, nodding. "True, this isn't as fun as kicking in doors and snatching bad guys out of their beds in the middle of the night, but that was my life back then." He shook his head. "I'm a different man now."

Wes chuckled as he shook his head. "Bullshit," he said as he walked off.

Ezra just watched as the other man walked back down the bar, thinking the same thing. *Bullshit.*

Chapter Three

Winnie stepped into the cabin thinking the place a little too quaint for her tastes. Why Deran insisted on this community for whatever scheme he had in mind was beyond her. It was funny that he wasn't staying there, as well. She wasn't even sure if the residents of Bull Creek would fall for his plan, giving him the information he needed, whatever that was. He hadn't shared much with her, so she wasn't even sure what information they were supposed to be gathering. When it was all said and done, it could very well prove to be a wasted trip. The paranormal world didn't necessarily fall for their lies as much as the human world did, simply because the supernatural had powers of their own and would be able to tell whether or not something was legit. They had never gone after other paranormals before. In her eyes, this was a waste of time and energy.

And then there was the whole issue with Mattox. That had been a surprise, and one she could have done without. She didn't like that they were there to work for him, or that he intended to harm someone for a past offense. Deran hadn't said much other than someone in Bull Creek had killed Mattox's brother. She had seen his brother killed, saw the black bear who did it, even though at the time, she was too busy trying to save her own skin. When it came to Mattox doling out his own brand of retribution, the man didn't possess a conscience. That she knew. The man had killed dozens of people and had no qualms about wiping out entire families for the slightest offense to his ego. She had seen him do it, had heard of the devastation left in the wake of his displeasure. Since then, she had avoided any dealings with the man. She had thought Deran had, as well, so it had surprised her when he mentioned Mattox's name. She supposed she should have known better. Once Mattox had you in his grip, he never let go. She was foolish to think it had been different with her. With that man involved, however, things just became more complicated. A hell of a lot more complicated.

She sighed as she picked a box up off the floor and set it on the island, flipping the flaps open so she could start pulling out the contents. She wasn't even sure how Deran had landed them a cabin in this town. It's not like there was a real estate office in the area or a welcome center of sorts. As she told Deran earlier, there were only three businesses that she had seen: a diner, a gas station, and a bar. And, if she was honest, only the bar looked like it would pass any type of health inspection. Of course, from what she could tell, it had just been rebuilt within the last couple of months. The other businesses have been around since Christ came out of the tomb, it seemed. She had stepped inside Gracie's Diner when she first arrived and then turned around and walked right back out because there was just so much grease embedded on the floor and clinging to the air that she had to take three showers once she returned to her cabin just to feel clean.

As she reached into the box and pulled out a stack of plates, she heard a knock on the door. Glancing up, she cocked a brow, wondering who in the world would be knocking on her door way out in the middle of no-fucking-where. There was no way one of those religious people had found her out here to tell her about their god.

Reaching out with her senses, she felt the presence of another witch standing on her porch. Setting the plates on the island that separated the kitchen from the living room, she moved around it toward the front of the cabin, curiosity filling her.

Opening the door, she saw a short, dark-haired woman standing there, a smile on her face that reached her deep blue eyes as she stared up at Winnie. She held a small plate of cookies in her hands. "May I help you?" Winnie asked, tilting her head to the side slightly as she studied the other woman.

"I just wanted to welcome you to Bull Creek," the shorter lady said as she handed the tray of sweets to Winnie. "My name's Adira. My boyfriend, Dimitri, is the alpha of this community. We like to greet everyone when they first arrive, make sure they don't need help with anything." She shrugged, still smiling. "So, how are things going? You getting along all right? Anything you need?"

Winnie laughed as she opened the door, holding the tray of cookies in one hand as she gestured for Adira to enter the cabin. "I appreciate it," she said. "I'm Winnie. Pleased to meet you. So far, everything seems to be going all right. Of course, I'm still unpacking so anything can happen."

The other woman laughed softly, as she nodded, stopping in the living room and turning around to face Winnie. However, Winnie noticed the woman scanning the cabin as she did. "Did you bring a lot of stuff with you?"

Winnie shook her head. "Not really," she told the other woman as she gestured for Adira to take a seat at the table. "Would you like some tea or coffee perhaps."

"That would be great, if I'm not taking you from anything," Adira said as she moved over to the small wooden table. "I know how hectic it can be moving into a new place." She slid into a chair, spinning slightly so she could keep an eye on Winnie, something Winnie was quite used to as it turned out. Everyone seemed to want to keep her in their sights lately.

Winnie simply smiled as she moved to the kitchen to fix a couple of cups of tea. "I tend to move around a lot," she said as she filled a kettle full of water. It was one of the first things she unpacked when she arrived. "Hence why I keep my material possessions kind of limited. Less to worry about that way." She gestured out the window, smiling over at Adira. "Besides, anything I truly need can be found out there. Right?"

Adira nodded, smiling as she followed Winnie's gesture toward the window. "True, but not many people outside of here think that way. Do you spend a lot of time in nature?"

Winnie bit down on a giggle as she realized she was being interrogated without it looking like an interrogation. The town's alpha probably assumed she would open up more to a woman more so than a man and sent his girlfriend to check out the new freak in town. She sighed as she set the kettle to boil and then moved to grab two teacups. "I'm a witch," she told the other woman as she stuffed two infusers with tea. "I prefer being out in nature to being indoors, to be honest. I have a better connection with the elements than I do with people most times."

Adira chuckled, nodding. "I can relate to that. The elements give us everything we need. And sometimes, people," she took a deep breath, shrugging. "Well, sometimes, they just give us everything we hate."

The teakettle whistled, announcing the water was hot, and Winnie turned back around to the stove. "That they do," she said softly. "That they do."

As she poured the tea, she thought about Deran being one of those people that gave her stuff she hated. She didn't want to be mixed up with anything that had Mattox's name on it. The man was simply too unpredictable for her tastes. Deran should have warned her; although, she could understand why he didn't. If he had, she wouldn't be standing there right now.

She set Adira's cup in front of her and then took her own seat. "How long have you lived here?"

The other woman pulled her teacup closer, the steam curling in slow circles from the hot tea. "Just over a year," she said, lifting the cup and blowing across the top. "I was asked to come out here by a witch back in Draven Falls when Dimitri was having some issues with a pack of coyote shifters." She smiled over at Winnie, giving her a one-shoulder shrug. "It was a rough start, but we won in the end."

Winnie nodded, pulling her own cup closer but not picking it up. "I spoke to the elements when I first arrived. The ground showed me the history of this place. Your little community hasn't had an easy go of it from what I could tell. I was impressed with the way you handled it, though. Everyone seemed pretty resourceful."

"We've had a battle or two, true, but for the most part, we're an easy-going bunch. We're also extremely loyal to each other. You'll find that most of the people here have gone through their own private battles. It's kind of what makes them protective of each other." Adira lifted her teacup and took a tentative sip. She arched her brows, nodding. "Lavender. Nice choice," she said, lowering the cup.

"And do you usually visit newcomers to warn them about the loyalty of your little community?" Winnie asked, not really wanting to start off on a bad foot with this woman, but tired of the questions and sneaky little lectures.

Adira shook her head as she wrapped her hands around her cup. "You misunderstand me. I'm not telling you this as a warning but as a promise. Usually, Alanna and Eve do the whole Welcome Wagon bit, so you're probably not getting the best experience. However, people come to Bull Creek because it's a safe haven for wandering souls. No one sticks their nose into anyone's past, even though you're free to talk about whatever you feel comfortable sharing. Of course, when you need something, everyone in this little town will have your back." She shrugged, a soft smile decorating her lips. "I was making you an assurance, not a threat, I promise you."

Winnie felt the blush warm her cheeks at the rebuke and realized she had judged the woman based on Deran's goals, assuming she had already been discovered. "I'm sorry," she said. "I tend to color new circumstances from past experiences. A habit I need to break, I know."

Adira offered her a sympathetic smile. "Well, I'm here anytime you need to talk, and whatever you share stays between us." She shifted slightly in her seat, her smile growing bigger. "To be honest, I wanted to come out and see you because I could sense there was another witch in the area. It'll be nice having someone to share things with who actually understands them. Dimitri just stares at me with glazed eyes whenever I talk about magic."

Winnie chuckled, nodding. "Our world is unique, for sure. I

would like that, as well. Truly."

"Do you have any plans while you're here?"

Winnie hesitated for a moment, not sure how much she should reveal before she was ready to set up shop. Still, Adira might give her an inkling as to whether or not her plans would be welcomed in Bull Creek. "Well, I used to tell fortunes back in St. Augustine. I kind of hoped to set up shop here and do the same thing. Of course, I didn't see too many businesses for rent here, so my plans may have to be altered some."

"Well, you could always set up shop here to start out," Adira suggested, gesturing to Winnie's cabin. "Just get word out about what you're doing, so people know where to find you. Wes, who runs Everglades, might let you have a table in the corner, as well. To be honest, Dimitri and I have talked about getting a few more businesses close by so we didn't have to travel so far to get things. We've just been worried it would detract from the quietness of the area, however. It's a catch-22."

Winnie nodded. "It is quiet and out of the way. It's one of the things that appealed to me when I discovered it. I can see why you wouldn't want it to change."

They talked for a while longer, each sharing their experiences with magic. Winnie asked about the wards she discovered earlier, and Adira told her about Bane Kastner and his pack of coyotes who tried to run anyone who wasn't a shifter out of Bull Creek. Eventually, they finished their tea, and the young witch said she had to go.

"However, several of us usually hit Everglades at night," Adira said as she reached the front door. "Feel free to pop in, and I'd be happy to introduce you to the crew. There really are some great people here. I'm sure you'll like them."

"Thanks," Winnie said, opening the door. "I'll see how I feel after unpacking all these boxes." She chuckled glancing back at the mess in her living room. "It's not a lot, I know, but it is tedious, even with the help of magic."

Adira chuckled, nodding. "I've been there. I don't envy you. Well, if I can do anything, just let me know. And welcome to Bull Creek."

Winnie watched as the dark-haired woman disappeared down her dirt driveway, wondering how welcoming Adira would be once she discovered their true motives for being in her quiet community.

Chapter Four

"Aren't these games a little outdated?" Josh Rayburn asked as he helped Ezra unload one of the massive video games from the back of the truck.

Jake Goodman just laughed as he guided them down the runway. "That's what makes them classics. They're perfect."

"But why do we need them?" Josh persisted. "I mean, you added the pool tables and some new dart boards. Don't you think that's enough to drive in traffic to the bar? This is just going to make the place crowded."

"I asked him the same thing," Noel Hastings said as she stood there, her hands on her curvaceous hips, the slight breeze pulling at her blond hair. "He just said they weren't for the guests."

Jake shrugged, showing no remorse for his desire to add to the entertainment of the bar. "That's right. They're for me. Who doesn't love Galaga and Asteroids? They were my favorite games when my father introduced me to the old video games. Oh, and I have Pac-Man and Space Invaders. Love those, but Asteroids is my all-time favorite."

"But there's no graphics, no pizazz. It's just a flat triangle shooting around the screen breaking up big rocks into smaller rocks until they disappear," Josh said, disbelief all over his face.

Ezra bit down on the laugh that threatened to burst past his lips. "The man likes what he likes," he said with a slight shrug. "Who can blame him for that?"

Josh shot a glance at Ezra, scowling. "I can. I want 3D graphics, bloodshed, and plenty of violence in my games. I want it to feel real."

"We've had enough of that around here this year," Noel said. "I'll take the simple games, thanks."

This time, Ezra did laugh. "Looks like it's just you and your Xbox in your room."

Josh made a dramatic sigh. "As if Alanna would let me. She hates those games with a passion. I think they give her nightmares."

"Did someone say games?"

Everyone turned as a tall man with short-cropped dark hair approached. Ezra sniffed the air, a habit from his days with Para-Force whenever a situation seemed to change, or a newcomer suddenly appeared. He narrowed his eyes as the other man drew nearer, the thick scent of magic in the air.

"Arcade games, to be exact," Jake said as he crossed the asphalt to shake the man's hand. "My name's Jake. I help run Everglades. I haven't seen you around here before. New to town?"

The other man shook Jake's hand as Josh and Ezra finished unloading the game. "Deran Sheridan, and I'm staying just up the road for the time being at that small motel. This seemed the closest bar around, and I was curious if you held poker games here."

Ezra watched as Jake's eyes lit up at the mention of another opportunity to bring people to the bar. If the man wasn't careful, he'd have Wes in a snit before long. Bull Creek was a small community, and the residents preferred their solitude. The town was supposed to be a sanctuary for those who were lost, after all, tired of the way the world treated them. If Jake kept attempting to draw in bigger crowds, he'd piss off his loyal customer base, which would piss Wes off. Ezra hated to think what that would do to the triad, especially to Noel who would find herself stuck in the middle, and not in the way she was accustomed.

"I'm not sure how many poker players there are around here," Jake said. "But we could give you a table and see who shows up." He glanced over at Noel, and the look on her face seemed to cause him to pause. "Of course, I'll need to run it by my partners first. Get their approval."

Noel simply rolled her eyes as she moved to the ramp at the back of the truck.

Ezra chuckled as he walked by Jake, whispering, "Smart man."

Jake nodded but said nothing.

"I'd appreciate that," Deran said as he reached into his back pocket and pulled out his wallet. Opening it, he pulled out a business card and handed it over to Jake. "Just give me a call once you find out." He glanced back at the bar, his lips pressed into a thin line as he nodded. "I love the look of the place." He turned back to Jake. "I've always preferred smaller, rustic bars to those new-fangled clubs. It's one of the reasons I avoid Las

Vegas and Biloxi. Call me old-fashioned."

Jake chuckled, slipping his hands to hips. "I can relate, being from a big city myself. I always sought out the smaller places. The clientèle seemed friendlier and less likely to be after anything but a good time. That's the way I prefer my bars."

"Same here," Deran said, nodding. "Well, I'll let you get back to it. I just wanted to introduce myself, as I said." He turned, glancing around at the others until his gaze fixed on Ezra. "I'm sure I'll be seeing you around." He gave a quick nod and then turned and walked off, heading to the front of the bar, where Ezra assumed the man's car was.

Ezra leaned on the top of the video game, staring after the man. "Anyone else find it odd that he came back here, instead of going inside to ask about his poker game?" He turned and glanced at Jake. "He can't see us from the road, so how did he even know we were here? We weren't making that much noise to draw attention to ourselves."

Josh shrugged. "Stop looking for trouble where none exists. I think working for that old squad of yours is making you yearn for the old days. Now, come on, let's get these games inside, so I can kick your ass at them."

"Hey, they're my games," Jake said, almost sounding like he was pouting. "I get first dibs."

"Oh, no," Josh said, as he leaned back on the game and started to wheel it inside. "We're doing this for free, so we get first dibs. Consider it part of our payment."

"I thought you were getting paid in beer," Jake said as he grabbed the handles of another hand truck and wheeled one of the other games inside, as well.

"Right," Josh said. "That's why I said *part* of our payment. Beer and first dibs on the game. It's the price for working on hump day when I should be doing something else, if you know what I mean."

"You can't renegotiate halfway through a job," Jake called after Josh's departing back.

"Are you kidding me? That's the best time to renegotiate."

Ezra ignored the bantering between the other two men as he stared off after Deran, who was just now disappearing around the corner of the bar.

"Something wrong?" Noel asked as she stepped up beside him, focusing her attention in the same direction he did.

"When I was with Para-Force, I always got this uneasy feeling up my neck whenever something didn't sit right in my craw," Ezra said, still staring off as if he could see the man. His bear prowled within, spinning in uneasy circles. "I've got that feeling now." He stared for a couple of more moments and then shrugged, blowing out a breath as if trying to shake his uneasy feeling. "What do I know? Josh is probably right, and I'm just allowing this assignment for Julian to get me wired." He pulled back on the hand truck, hoisting the Space Invaders game backward, and then started toward the back door of Everglades. "I think I could use that beer Jake promised me."

Noel laughed as she followed him. "I'll get you all set up while you put Jake's new toys in place."

Ezra chuckled as she walked around him and opened the back door. "What is it with him and his toys?"

She shrugged as he passed her, pushing the video game over the small threshold and into the bar. "He likes what he likes, and he just wants it around him. I can't say I blame him. After all, he left the big city for Bull Creek. Not exactly an upgrade."

"That's not true," he said as she closed the door. "He left his hometown for you and Wes. That's definitely an upgrade in my opinion."

"Well, thank you, Mr. Havlin. I'll make sure it's one of our better beers for that one."

"He was going to give me cheap beer?" Ezra asked as he moved through the bar. "Typical."

Noel just laughed as she left him for the big wooden bar toward the front of Everglades.

He wheeled the video game through the bar, passing the high-tops and the smaller round tables with wooden chairs circling them. Everglades had been destroyed a few months back by The Order of Wardens, trashing the inside and spray-painting vulgar sayings on the walls inside and out. As Jake helped them fix the place up, he used his big city mindset to add to the decor and offerings, trying to go a little more upscale, even though he said he preferred the smaller places. The man had expensive tastes. Wes insisted on keeping Everglades' rustic charm, however. He didn't want it to stand out, but rather blend in with the woods around them. The only other change that everyone agreed on was the parking lot. It was no longer the gravelly, bumpy mess it once was, but now was covered with asphalt for a smoother ride and marked off parking spaces, mainly to keep Josh from shoving his car wherever he wanted in his rush to get inside. They did a great job of maintaining the same feel the bar held already while giving it the uplift to keep it from growing stagnant, a balance that Ezra thought revealed the two personalities of the men who owned it. It was one of Ezra's favorite places.

"Oh, come on, man," Josh said as Ezra wheeled the machine into the back part of the bar. "I should at least get a go at one of these things first. Hell, you have four of them."

"You whine a lot," Jake said shaking his head as he plugged in the Asteroids machine. He stood, staring over at Josh for a moment as Ezra put the machine he wheeled into a corner. "Fine. Have a go at that one." Jake pointed to the Galaga machine, smiling. "Don't say I never did anything nice for you."

Josh nodded, a cocky grin on his face as he turned toward the machine, cracking his knuckles. "Now, we're talking."

Ezra leaned on the machine he just finished plugging in and stared over at his friend, who was simply staring at the machine in front of him, his brows pinched together in confusion.

"Um, Jake," Josh said, tilting his head slightly as he studied the machine, every once in a while pushing a button or using the lever. "How do you get this thing to turn on?"

Jake chuckled as he patted Josh on the back. "You have to put a quarter in it." And then the man walked off, shaking his head as he left a trail of laughter behind him.

Josh turned as the other man walked away. "Are you kidding me? We have to pay to play these ancient games? That's just rude!"

Ezra laughed as he pointed to the back of the bar. "Come on, cheapskate. We have another game to fetch."

Josh sighed as he followed Ezra back out of the bar. "Can you believe that? He wants us to give him money. We can play these games on our phones. Why would we pay him to play them?"

"I don't know," Ezra said as he pushed the back door open. "Maybe because it's a business, and that's how they keep the doors open." He shook his head. "It's only a quarter."

"I don't have any quarters," Josh said. "Alanna steals them, so she can put them in that damn jukebox whenever she comes here. Now, I'm going to have to figure out how to hide them."

"You have such a rough life," Ezra said, chuckling.

"I bet no one steals your quarters," Josh said as they reached the truck.

Ezra paused at the back of the vehicle, putting his hand on Josh's shoulder, and stopping him before he could crawl into the truck. "Be thankful you have someone who can take your quarters. That means you have someone in your life." He squeezed his friend's shoulder and then climbed into the back of the truck, a tight fist around his heart.

Chapter Five

Why the hell did I have to come all the way out here?" Winnie said as she glanced around the dingy motel room. "This place is a dump. Why didn't you just get a cabin, like I did? I thought the whole point was to get close to these people." She would never understand Deran's approach to things. The man seemed to want to achieve certain goals but never wanted to get close to the flames of his own games.

"Because, I prefer a little distance between me and my marks," he told her as he handed her a bottle of water. "I've had to make a run for it too many times to trust to fate too much. I'd be trapped in that backwoods town. They only have one main road going in or out, or did you fail to scout out your surroundings?"

She twisted the cap off her bottle and downed half its contents. When she finished, she wiped her mouth with the back of her hand, blowing out a breath through her nose. "I scouted everything when you told me that's where I would be staying, probably the same way you did, with my magic. I know all the roads and creeks and trees. I won't be trapped. There may only be one road, but there are plenty of ways in and out of there." She sighed as she plopped down on the bed, her frustration filling her. "I still don't know why we're doing this. You should have told me about Mattox's involvement. I assume he's the reason we're gathering this information, which you also haven't told me about, by the way."

"What? And have you walk away from this?" He shook his head. "I'm smarter than that. I know you don't like him, but it's what the job is. We don't get to pick and choose."

"Wrong," she said. "You didn't give me a chance to pick and choose. There's a difference. Don't ever make a decision like this for me again."

He cocked a brow at her. "Are you threatening me?" He chuckled. "Oh, Winnie, I am so much stronger than you. That would be a foolish thing to do. Besides, Mattox owns you just as he owns me. Just because he ignores you most of the time, doesn't mean he's forgotten about you."

She blew out a breath as she crossed her ankles, holding her bottle with both hands between her legs. "I don't care," she told him, and meant it, even though she knew it could be a mistake. "I won't be tricked like this again. It doesn't matter what you do to me. Mattox is dangerous. I won't be mixed up in his chaos again."

Deran narrowed his eyes at her, a sinister smile curving his lips. "You'll be mixed up in anything he damn well plans on you being mixed up in. Never forget that, or you'll be on the same shit list as the one he came here to kill."

"And just who is that?" she demanded to know. "You still haven't told me the whole of why we're here. Seems there's two different agendas. You want to steal the land and create a place for your coven to live, a coven that doesn't even exist yet. He wants revenge on the person who killed his brother. What does one have to do with the other? I don't get it."

"They only have to do with each other in the fact that Mattox has promised me this land once he's accomplished his mission." He walked over to the dresser, leaning back on it as he crossed his arms over his chest. "Perfect timing if you ask me. Means we have his help, just as he has ours, and we both get what we want in the end."

"I don't kill people," she told him, her voice low, almost as if she was ready for the fight she knew brewed between them. "I never have, and I don't intend on starting now, even for Mattox. So, I hope you have another plan for me, because I won't participate in what I've heard so far."

"You just do your part," he warned her. "And perhaps things will work out that you won't have to cross your pathetic moral code. You're all right stealing from these people, but not to help Mattox find justice for his brother."

"I remember Mattox's brother well," she said, clutching tighter to her water bottle. "He wasn't a nice man. He sold women and children. Hell, he would have sold me, as well."

"He didn't sell you, as I recall," Deran said, staring at her with his cold eyes. 'I would think you owe him for that."

Winnie shuddered, the thought of that day rippling through her memory, leaving a dark stain.

She huddled in the back of the truck, her knees pulled up to her chest, her arms wrapped around them. The small bay area was filled with the sniffling and crying of the others, kids clutching to their mothers, women huddled in on themselves as they whimpered from where they had been beaten. Mattox and his brother, Jace, had captured each and every one of them, knocking them around as they hauled them inside a warehouse to await the next leg of their journey. Once they had enough victims, the truck arrived, and the brothers, gorilla shifters, transformed into their animals in front of the women and children to scare them into obedience as they told them to get into the truck. One woman tried to escape, and Mattox's brother snatched her by the neck and threw her against the corner of the truck, breaking her back. Everyone else scrambled into the back of the truck just to avoid another attack and quite possibly their death.

The vehicle bounced as they drove, and Winnie could tell they took the back roads, off the main highways to avoid detection or possibly being stopped. The air in the back of the truck was stifling, sweat beading on her forehead and dripping into her eyes. Most of the others were covered in dirt, some bleeding from cuts obtained during their capture. Winnie didn't know any of them, all of them strangers to each other except for the kids who were taken with their mothers. She wondered if their husbands had been with them at their abduction and, if so, what had happened to them. Dead, more than likely.

She swiped at her eyes, tears she never meant to shed falling as she steeled her resolve. She would get out of this. They made one mistake. They didn't know who she was and never took the time to find out, assuming she was just another weak female.

Closing her eyes, she reached out with her senses, searching for the elements around her. With a slow, steady breath, she called out to the air surrounding her, bringing it into herself. She then found the water from her sweat and the sweat of the others *and called forth its power. Dirt clung to the victims in the truck, and she reached out for it, pulling its magic from their bodies. She swirled the magic around, turning it into a weapon as she used it to seek out any weaknesses in the truck.*

The bay door had a slight crack around the bottom from where it hadn't closed all the way, and Winnie sent her magic there to wait. As soon as she thought it safe, she would spring the door, shoving it upward and then throw the people out the back. She would not allow them to take these women and children.

The sound of the brakes squealing reached her ears as she felt the force of her body falling to the side slightly as the truck came to a stop. Now was her chance. She leaped to her feet, stretching her arm out as she shoved a blast of her magic at the door. Jerking her hand upward, the bay door flew open, revealing a dark road behind them. She didn't wait. She wrapped the people up in her power and hurled them from the truck, each landing on the ground as she raced to follow them.

The people stood, staring around, confusion on their faces.

What the hell? "Run!" she screamed as she leaped down from the truck.

However, before her feet could hit the ground, something punched her in the chest, shoving her backward into the tailgate of the vehicle. Pain shot through her as white stars dotted her vision. With a deep breath, she struggled to get up, but felt a giant hand grip the top of her head.

Opening her eyes, she stared into the dark orbs of a gorilla, Mattox's brother from what she remembered. He roared, shaking her head, saliva dripping from his teeth. When he looked back at her, fury raged behind his eyes. She was going to die; she knew it. Hopefully, some of the others had managed to escape at least.

Gunfire ripped through the air, causing Winnie to clench her eyes as she shrunk in on herself.

"*A noble attempt,*" *Mattox said as he walked around the truck, his gun aimed at the ground.* "*Sad, of course, but noble.*" *He cocked his head as he stared at her, his eyes narrowed.* "*A witch. I should have looked into you more closely. I might just have a use for your power.*" *He squatted down, so he could look her in the eyes.* "*That's the only reason you're alive right now, by the way, so I wouldn't push me. Keep your magic to yourself if you want to live through this.*" *As he shoved himself back to his feet, he turned and glared at the others.*

His brother released Winnie, shoving her back into the tailgate, so that she hit her head on the metal frame as he shifted back to his human form. He grunted as his bones snapped and popped, his head twisting as it shrunk from the black gorilla to his natural form.

Once he was done, he turned back to Winnie, glaring at her with a deep-seated hatred in his eyes. "*That was foolish,*" *he snarled, his upper lip twisted up in a sneer. Naked, he walked over to his brother, snatching the gun from his hand as he turned back to Winnie.*

She froze, gripping the ground with her palms as she watched him walk back to her, his face twisted in fury. She was about to die. She knew it. It didn't matter what Mattox said. His brother was going to shoot her right there.

"*Don't do it,*" *Mattox said, sighing.* "*I have uses for her. We can team her up with Deran. He's been looking for a new partner. Besides, we may need her powers one day.*"

Jace roared up at the sky, his arms shaking with his anger. Spinning, he aimed the gun at the others.

Winnie yelled, reaching out with her arm to stop him, not caring that it would seal her fate.

However, she was too late. The gun ripped the silence, and a second later a ten-year-old boy fell to the ground, his body jerking backward, and spinning him around. The man then shot the boy's mother as she raced toward her son. Her body fell to the earth just a few feet away from the little boy.

Jace spun back around to Winnie, fire in his eyes. "You pull that shit again, and I'll kill them all. I don't care what we lose. You use your magic, and people will die. Remember that." He shoved the gun into Mattox's stomach and stormed off around the side of the truck.

Winnie glanced out at the others, everyone standing there, mothers holding their children behind them as if they could protect them. They couldn't, of course, and Winnie knew it. Not against Mattox and his brother. These men didn't care what they did or who they hurt. They were soulless beings, hellbent on their own evil ambitions.

Her entire body shook as Mattox motioned for the others to get back into the truck, waving them into motion with his gun. Winnie sat there, staring, numb. She had wanted to help, wanted to save these people, but she had only managed to get a couple of them killed.

Mattox walked over to her, holding his hand out to help her to her feet as if he weren't the murderous bastard she knew him to be. Once she was on her feet, he jerked her around, shoving her toward his car. "You'll ride with me," he told her. "I think we need to talk about your future."

He shoved her into the back of the vehicle and then slid into the front seat himself, motioning for the driver to get going. Just as they pulled away, Jace climbed up into the passenger side of the truck's cab, and then a roar ripped the night air.

Winnie glanced behind her, watching as several different animals rushed the truck, a gorilla jumping onto the roof as a capuchin monkey swung to the back of the vehicle. Jace climbed out of the cab, ready to shift and fight, she assumed, but just then a giant black bear raced out of the darkness, leaping up and dragging Jace to the ground before he could shift again.

The driver of Mattox's car stopped, obviously ready to go back and help the others, but just then another shape flew across the windshield causing an even darker shadow over the car.

"Drive!" Mattox screamed, as he watched the scene behind them unfold.

There were too many shifters, and not enough of his men. Winnie just sat there, staring as she saw the bear drag Mattox's brother into the high grass on the side of the road. Jace's screams could be heard as they drove away.

Mattox turned to her, glaring. "This is your fault," he snarled at her. "Because of your little stunt, we were found. Don't think I'll forget this." He glanced over her shoulder as the bear raced back out onto the road, shifting into a thick-bodied man. "Nor will I forget him."

"No, he didn't sell me," she said to Deran. "What he did was much, much worse." She shuddered again as the memory faded, remembering quite well the determination on Mattox's face when he saw the bear shift back to his human form. And now that man was here in Bull Creek, obviously, which is why she was once again stuck working for the monster who turned her into what she was now—a common thief and con artist.

Chapter Six

Ezra stepped into Everglades, the music from the jukebox filling the place, a noisy din over the conversations. Josh and Alanna already took up residence at a high-top table in the back, and Ezra spotted Dimitri and Adira out on the dance floor. Waving at Wes as he passed the bar, he weaved his way through the tables until he slid up to where the others stood. "Anyone else here?" he asked as he leaned on the wooden tabletop.

Alanna nodded. "Those two on the dance floor, and Eve and Arlin are checking out the new video games. Seems Arlin's never played Pac-Man, and Eve is determined to get her name in the highest score slot."

"I think I overheard a bet between them," Josh said. "But I'm not sure if I should say who gets what when it's all said and done. Some things should be left between couples, even here in Bull Creek."

Ezra chuckled, nodding as he flagged down Noel. "Is that even possible?"

Noel saddled up to the side of the table, laughing. "I doubt it. Most of us have hearing that dogs envy. What can I get you to drink?"

"Hell, I can hear what goes on in most cabins no matter how hard I try not to," Ezra said. "I'm thinking of getting some of those noise canceling earbuds to protect my sanity." He shook his head, chuckling. "I'll just take a beer, thanks. Whatever's on tap."

"I love a man who isn't picky," she said, giggling as he walked off.

"How has Wes taken to Jake's new toys?" Ezra asked the others as he leaned on the table.

"I still don't think he likes them," Alanna said. "He prefers quiet bars without all the fuss. I think the pool tables were a big adjustment for him, as well."

"Yeah, but I'm sure he likes the customers those things bring in," Josh said. "Means more money in his pocket."

"Someone has money in their pockets?" Dimitri asked as he and Adira slid up to the table. "Who's the lucky bastard?"

"We're talking about Wes and the video games," Alanna said.

The others joined in the conversation as Ezra glanced around. Alanna and Josh. Dimitri and Adira. In the back were Eve and Arlin, and then there was the triad, Wes, Noel, and Jake. He was the odd man out. Over the past year and a half, everyone had discovered their mate, most due to life bringing them who was meant to be in their life during all the chaos that had descended upon their little community. So, where was his? He hadn't realized how much he wanted someone in his life until all his friends were paired up with someone. Even Josh and Alanna knew who they were meant to spend the rest of their life with, even though they hadn't consummated their mating call, yet. Did another catastrophe have to happen in Bull Creek before he found his soulmate? He hoped not, but if that's what it took, he would gladly suffer another battle to simply not be alone anymore.

"So, I met the lady who took over Marilyn Bowman's old cabin," Adira said. Marilyn Bowman had been a witch who lived in Bull Creek before Dimitri and Josh were sent to replace the first alpha, Neal Porter. Bane ran her out, along with the other witches, and no one had taken her cabin since she escaped. From what Adira heard, the witch wound up in St, Augustine, somehow working with a detective to solve crimes. Adira wasn't exactly sure how a witch could help in that capacity, but according to Agatha Rochester back in Draven Falls, Marilyn did some amazing work. "I even invited her to come out and meet some of you. She seems nice enough. A witch, so it'll be nice to have someone to talk magic with."

"I talk magic with you," Dimitri said, his brows furrowed, his hurt look obvious.

"You babble as best you can and listen to me talk about magic," Adira said, giggling. "You don't know the first thing about it, but I love that you try." She leaned in on his shoulder, kissing his neck. "She'll be someone I can get specific with. She actually said she came across my old wards." She glanced at Ezra and Josh. "The ones you two helped me put out when Bane tried to run the humans out of Bull Creek. Their magic has faded, of course, but it still told her of my presence here."

"Is that safe?" Dimitri asked. "Could someone use those

stones to hurt you or track you?"

She shook her head. "Not likely. They might know I exist, but they wouldn't reveal my exact location. They would need something of my DNA on them still to use a locator spell, and I'm sure the elements have wiped them clean by now."

"Still, perhaps we should round them up and dispose of them properly," Dimitri said. "I don't like that she knew about you from those wards."

Adira slid her arm around his, smiling up into his eyes. "If that's what you want, love. We'll go out tomorrow and look for them."

Dimitri nodded, and Ezra noticed the man dropped the subject after that. He couldn't blame the alpha, though. Too many men had swarmed Bull Creek looking to cause harm. If there was a way to use Adira's wards to cast a spell on her, he didn't doubt that someone would figure it out. He had seen enough with Para-Force to know there was no limit to the depths people would go to in their depravity.

"So what brought the lady to our little haven?" Josh asked, lifting his beer to his lips.

Adira gave him a knowing look. "You know damn well we don't ask those questions. If people want to open up to us, then they're free to do so, but we don't pry. That's what makes our little town work. People feel safe with their secrets."

"But some have used those secrets to hurt us." Josh placed his beer to his lips and tilted the bottle up, draining half its contents.

"True," Dimitri said. "But that doesn't mean I'm changing our policy on no busybodies."

Josh just nodded but said nothing as he glanced over at Ezra. He knew what his friend was thinking. If Josh hadn't stuck his nose into Ezra's business, he'd still be living in a tent at the edge of town. He wanted nothing to do with anything happening around him at the time or in the world in general, having left Para-Force in a cloud of guilt and shame for failing to save a small child. He couldn't live with his failure and had simply slid into anonymity, until Josh and Lainie stumbled upon him while escaping Miles Hemingway who was after Lainie for running away from his marriage proposal. Luckily, Ezra had been there to help save her, taking a bullet himself that was meant for her. Sometimes, you needed someone to butt into your life to keep you from traveling a dark path. Ezra smiled as he dipped his head slightly at Josh, and the other man repeated the gesture, both knowing what the other was thinking.

Noel returned with his beer, asking if anyone else needed anything before returning to the bar.

"So, is she here for good, or just passing through?" Dimitri asked.

"Well, she knew you sent me to her," Adira said with a chuckle. "But, I couldn't tell what her intentions were. She seemed to insinuate that she moves around a lot, which has to suck. People need to lay down roots, I believe. She's pretty perceptive, I'll give you that. She used her powers to read the elements, which is how she found the ancient wards. I'm not sure how powerful she is, another reason I wanted her to come out tonight, so I could see her a little more relaxed. I could tell she was on guard this afternoon."

"Wonder what that was about?" Alanna asked, cocking her head to the side slightly.

"Because another witch invaded her space more than likely," Adira said with a slight shrug.

"How's your research going for Julian," Dimitri asked Ezra.

"Not too bad," Ezra told him. "It's crazy the things people will do because they feel entitled to what's not theirs. There's a group out there stealing the hides off paranormals and selling them."

"That's rather gross," Alanna said, her face pinched with disgust.

"Well, well, well," Josh said as he glanced over Ezra's shoulder at something behind him. "That man who was here earlier just walked in. Wonder if Jake talked Wes into letting him start a poker game here."

"A poker game?" Dimitri asked, his brows furrowed as he glanced to where Josh looked.

Josh nodded. "Yeah, this man appeared while we were unloading the video games from the truck."

"Which was weird," Ezra said, cutting his friend off. "Because he didn't enter the bar once. It seemed like he came straight around the place to where we were, and it wasn't like we were making a lot of noise."

Josh shook his head. "You're just naturally suspicious."

"Perhaps," Ezra said with a shrug. "But being suspicious has saved my life more times than I can count."

"Anyway," Josh continued, ignoring his friend. "This guy, Deran if I remember correctly, asked Jake if he could start a poker game at Everglades. Said something like he preferred smaller bars to the big games in Las Vegas or Biloxi." He gestured to the man with an uplift of his chin. "Now he's here, so I wonder if he got the okay."

The man looked in their direction, recognizing Josh and Ezra apparently as he smiled and giving them a chin-lift greeting. He changed course and headed in their direction. Ezra wasn't sure why, but the hair on the back of his neck stood on end, and his bear growled inside, pacing in tight circles. Something about the approaching man set Ezra's teeth on edge, and he couldn't explain it. However, he learned a long time ago not to ignore his gut.

"How's everyone doing tonight?" Deran said as he neared their table. He then glanced around the bar, pressing his lips into a thin line as he nodded. "I could tell from the exterior that this would be my kind of place. I love the older establishments." He turned his attention back to the others. "They have more personality in my opinion."

"We like it," Dimitri said, extending his arm so he could shake the other man's hand. "I'm Dimitri, alpha of Bull Creek. How did you find our quiet little corner of the world?"

Deran shrugged, clasping his hands together as he leaned on the table. "I'm always on the lookout for a quiet place to hang my hat for a while. I caught wind of this place while traveling through Brighton Cove and thought I'd check it out."

Ezra shot Alanna a quick glance just in time to see her back stiffen as she stood straighter. "You're from Brighton Cove?" she asked.

Deran shook his head. "No, not really. I just passed through there, like I pass through a lot of places." He shrugged. "I've been passing through places since I was old enough to drive. I don't like the dust to settle around me for too long."

Ezra felt the red flags go up as he watched the other man, doing his best to keep his expression neutral. A person only moved around a lot for two reasons: they were running from something, or they were chased out of everywhere they parked their car. He wondered which was the case with Deran.

"Did you get permission for your poker game?" Josh asked, lifting his beer bottle once more.

Deran glanced around Everglades, searching for Jake, Ezra assumed. "No, I never did hear back from the owner of this place." He turned back to the others. "So, I thought I'd come and check it out for myself. See where I intended to host my game. Do any of you play poker?"

Dimitri and Josh both shook their heads, the ladies remaining quiet. Ezra shrugged slightly as he spun his bottle in slow circles. "It's been a while, but I've played a game or two. Not sure I'm up to your caliber, though."

"You haven't played me," Deran said, chuckling. "How do you know how I play?"

"You go around looking to start games," Ezra said, giving the man a pointed look. "You only do that if you know what you're doing. And, while it's true I haven't played you, I have played men like you. They all smiled the same way." He allowed his grin to grow as he watched the other man.

However, if Deran had been ruffled, he refused to show it. He simply smiled back at Ezra. "Well, then, I hope I get to match wits with you. I think it would be a challenge."

Ezra nodded. "I'm sure of it," he said, and somehow, he knew neither of them were talking about cards.

Chapter Seven

Winnie stood outside Gracie's Diner, still not sure this was the best place to set up a table. Still, the old lady who ran the place had offered her a spot outside, and Deran would be pissed if Winnie didn't take it. This was why he brought her there, after all. Her task was to mingle with the locals and find out whatever she could that would aid him in whatever it was he had planned. The problem was, she had no clue as to what he had planned, so she didn't know what information she was trying to pry out of people. It made no sense for him to be so closemouthed about things, especially if he wanted her help.

She set up a small card table just to the west of the front door, the smell of cheap gasoline from the convenience store that shared the same building almost over-powering. The air was humid, causing small strands of her hair to stick to her scalp. After placing some of her stones and crystals around the edges of the table, she laid out her tarot cards, along with a small wooden bowl for tips as she sat down in her metal folding chair. This had to be the worst set up she could remember using. Sure, she had worked fairs and carnivals, even private parties and as a busker out in Savannah, but this... This just seemed to be scraping the bottom of the barrel.

She sighed as she shuffled her tarot cards and waited. The memory of Mattox yesterday left her shook up, almost to the point of not wanting to do her part in Deran's little show. This is ridiculous. Why would witches who were used to the city and all of its comforts and conveniences ever want to live out here in the middle of nowhere? Sure, it had solitude, plenty of natural resources for their magic, and a clear path to all the elements a witch needed to replenish her strength. But there was more to life than just their magic. They needed interaction, people to assist in their journey, more than one diner. This place was quaint and peaceful, and the people she met so far seemed nice enough, but it lacked so many other things she was used to having in her life. She didn't want to drive forty minutes to get to a damn grocery store.

She set her tarot cards on the table, picking up part of the stack, and flipping the top card over and placing it at the top of her table. She then repeated the process until she had a six-card spread laid out in the shape of a star, one on top, two on bottom, two on either side, and one in the middle. She sat there, staring at the cards.

"Now, that looks interesting," a short blonde said as she approached the table.

Next to her walked a slender redhead, her hands stuffed into the pockets of her jeans. "First time I've seen a fortune teller in Bull Creek. We must be moving up on the map."

The blonde stepped up to the table, smiling as she glanced at the spread of cards on the table. "Good afternoon," she said. "My name's Eve, and this is Alanna. Interesting place to set up shop."

Winnie shrugged. "Not a lot of options, I'm afraid. The lady who owns the diner seemed happy enough to have me here, though, so I didn't want to pass up the chance. My name's Winnie, by the way."

"Oh, I'm sure," Eve said, smiling down at her. "Gracie's amazing. And you'll get plenty of traffic here. It's just odd to see someone out here practicing their craft, that's all."

"Been doing this long?" Alanna asked, studying the cards spread out on the table with her brows furrowed.

"In this town, no," Winnie said. "Telling fortune's, yes. I've been reading cards since I was in high school, and you'll forgive me if I don't tell you how long ago that was." She giggled as she said that last part, hoping to lighten the mood. She wasn't sure if the two women judged her or were just curious and making small talk. "Do you two live here?"

Eve nodded. "I've been here about two years, and Alanna a little longer than that. You staying around?"

Winnie nodded. "I have a cabin near the creek. Adira stopped by yesterday and introduced herself. I kind of think she was checking me out, to be honest."

"I wouldn't let it bother you," Alanna said. "We've had some trouble now and again, so everyone is a little cautious with newcomers. Still, it's a great group of people." She pointed to the cards. "Does this mean you're a witch?"

"I am," Winnie replied. "And am I allowed to ask about your connection to the paranormal world? Adira said something about everyone keeping their secrets, so I'm not sure what all is allowed to ask and what isn't."

"You can ask whatever you want," Eve said. "Just don't always expect an answer." She laughed at that other part as she sat down in the metal foldout chair across from Winnie. "I'm a human turned into a tiger shifter, thanks to my mate." She hooked her thumb back over her shoulder at Alanna. "She's a wolf shifter. Was the only one, actually, until last year when Rance arrived." She glanced back at her friend, her eyes narrowed. "I never did ask how it felt not to be the only one anymore."

"It feels the same as always," Alanna said, rolling her eyes. "It's not like we hang out and go to meetings together. There's not a wolf club."

Winnie watched the two banter back and forth for a few moments, noticing how close they were even though they picked on each other. Alanna seemed to have a rough edge to her while it was obvious Eve had endured a lot of emotional trauma while still maintaining her positive outlook on life. Winnie reached out slightly, trying to get an inside look into the women, but just as her senses reached the redhead, Alanna snapped her attention around, studying Winnie through narrowed slits.

"So, how much for a reading?" Eve asked, obviously not sensing that something had just happened.

"Twenty dollars," Winnie said as she kept her focus on Alanna, a smile on her face, hoping to put the other woman at ease. Still smiling, she turned back to Eve. "Would you like one? If you've never had one before, it truly is revealing."

Eve shrugged. "Sure." After pulling the twenty-dollar bill from her pocket, she settled more into her chair as the redhead stood behind her, a skeptical look on her face.

Winnie scooped up the cards she had laid out, adding them back to the stack before handing them over to the petite blonde.

"Shuffle them for me, as long as you want."

Eve took the cards and started to shuffle them, watching them as she did.

"The idea is to put your essence on the cards, so that they read what's inside of you. You'll get a better reading as you sit there, thinking about what it is you want to know."

"Just what do you want to know?" Alanna asked her friend, her head cocked to the side a little.

"Who knows?" Eve said, giggling as she finished shuffling the cards and handed them back to Winnie. "I've been wanting to gain a little direction in my life. With Arlin busy in St. Cloud, I seem to just wander around all day. It would be nice having a purpose of sorts."

"Practicing your knife throwing isn't purpose enough?" Alanna asked, grinning.

Winnie just smiled at the other ladies as she flipped the cards over in the same pattern as before. "This first card represents your current situation," she said, as she revealed the top card on the deck. The image was of a skeletal dragon standing in the underworld of shade and mist while holding a scythe. "Death. He reminds us that our lives hang by a tender thread. The hourglass you see on the side suggests we need to make the most of our lives because we only have so much time available to us. The egg on the other side of the card speaks of rebirth, telling us life must continue, one way or another. For you, I would think this means there is a clearing away of negative conditions, allowing you to find new and positive influences."

Eve glanced back at Alanna, smirking. "I wonder who the negative influence is."

Alana simply rolled her eyes.

Winnie flipped over the next card, announcing its name. "This is the Two of Cups. It represents either a new relationship starting or something exciting happening in a current relationship." Flipping over the third card, she said, "Ace of Wands. You see the dragon moving forward into action. This means you'll have a new initiative."

"Interesting names," Alanna deadpanned as she crossed her arms over her chest, standing there and staring down at the cards.

Winnie said nothing as she flipped over the next card. "The Empress. She is the queen over all creativity. It's telling us you need to cultivate your own creativity. Find something inside of you that you wish to do and then learn how to do it." The fifth card was the Queen of Swords, which showed a female dragon in a defensive position, ready to protect herself. "This shows you're a determined woman, but there might be something between you and others, whether a single someone or a group."

"Well, Arlin and I have been bickering a little bit about me growing bored and needing something to do," Eve said, studying the cards with pinched brows.

Alanna merely shrugged as Eve glanced back at her, and Winnie could tell the redhead wasn't fully buying what she heard.

Smiling, Winnie flipped over the final card. "The Sun," she said as they all stared at the lion's head surrounded by the zodiac resting on a Red Fire Dragon, which sits on the disk of Yin-Yang. "The disk represents eternal change. This speaks of growth in all aspects of your life. You shouldn't be afraid to step outside the box and find those things that bring you fulfillment and happiness." Winnie leaned back slightly, glancing over the cards one more time.

Eve sat across the table, staring at the cards, as well.

"Right now, the cards are showing a struggle, quite possibly where you were just talking about trying to find a purpose. This also shows some creativity in what you're trying to do." She glanced up at Eve. "Are you artistic?"

"Not that I'm aware of," Eve said, shaking her head. "I can't even draw stick men without messing them up."

"Artistic can be anything," Winnie told her. "Writing, singing, painting, crafting something. Maybe there's something there that draws your interest."

"Interesting," the petite blonde said. "I do like to do things with my hands." She glanced over her shoulder at Alanna. "Maybe that's it. I could start an online business with the things I create."

The redhead shrugged. "Worth a shot. What do you make?"

"I don't know," Eve said with a sigh. "But I'm sure I could make something."

As they sat there, Eve rambled nonstop about what she could make with her hands to sell online and even drafted a basic business plan there on the spot. She thanked Winnie as she stood, excitement now covering her face.

The redhead just shook her head, keeping her arms over her chest as they walked off, Eve fully invested now in what she just learned.

As Winnie watched them walk away she thought they were an interesting pair, bouncing off each other in their barbs and jests. However, Winnie could tell there was a deep bond there, something that only tragedy could forge. This town had seen more trauma than she first detected, and it shaped the course of Bull Creek's residents' lives.

"So, setting up shop already, I see. Good for you. Gives you a chance to get to know the people here."

A shiver ran up her spine as she heard Mattox's voice, and fear caused her muscles to clench as she watched him take the chair the blonde just vacated. Her body trembled, and she clutched to the stack of cards to try and hide her shaking. She glanced up at the other man but said nothing.

"What? Not happy to see me, Winifred?" Mattox asked, a fake pout turning down the corners of his lips. "You could hurt a man's feelings."

"What do you want, Mattox?" she asked as she glanced around at the people walking by, hoping no one would ever put the two of them together when all hell broke loose. And with Mattox, hell always broke loose.

"Deran shared some disturbing news with me," the man said as he picked up one of her stones, turning it over in his hands and studying it. She would definitely need to cleanse the stone now. "Seems you're not too happy about what we intend to do here." He glanced back at her, his eyes narrowing into dangerous slits. "Seems you don't appreciate that he kept my involvement from you. And here I thought we worked well together. Was I wrong?"

She took a slow, steadying breath as she stared across the table at him. "I don't like being kept in the dark," she said. "That's all. Deran led me to believe something that wasn't true and didn't give me all the facts when he asked for my help with this endeavor."

"You don't need all the facts, witch," Mattox sneered, his voice low and menacing. "You just need to do as you're fucking told. Don't forget that it's because of me you're even alive right now. You could have been dead, just like those others on that truck. Just like my brother. You're alive because of me, and you'll damn well show your appreciation by doing as you're told. If Deran tells me you're whining about what has to be done again, I'll make sure you regret it. These people need to be put in their place, one in particular. We're going to take this land, just as soon as Deran finds out what I need to finish the plan, and then we'll bring the others. This is going to be your new home, witch. Get used to it."

"These people have done nothing wrong," she said, softly, pleading with him. "They don't deserve what you want to do to them. They've been through enough. There's plenty of land elsewhere. Why here?"

He leaned across the table, narrowing his eyes even more. "Because when I hurt them, it'll hurt Ezra, and I intend on making him feel every ounce of the pain he caused me when he killed my brother. It's his punishment for getting involved in what was none of his business."

She nodded, another shiver rippling through her body. Whoever Ezra was, he had sealed the fate of everyone in Bull Creek. Mattox never failed to carry out whatever he intended to do, especially when it came to revenge. He would burn the community down just to punish one man.

"Now, find out what we need to know," Mattox said, leaning back in his chair, a smile toying at his lips. "Or, when I burn this backwoods hole in the ground to the soil where it resides, you'll burn along with them."

She watched as he slid out of his chair, standing, his gaze fixed onto hers. She merely nodded, afraid to say anything. She needed to get out of there before she found herself stuck between Mattox and Bull Creek. And she still didn't know what they expected her to find out.

Chapter Eight

Ezra sat on the ground, his back against a towering cypress as he stared out at Crabgrass Creek, a couple of mallards drifting across the surface, the sun's reflection on top of the rippling water. He felt a calmness every time he sat there, as if the water had healing powers for his soul. Of course, he knew Adira would tell him it actually did possess those qualities as one of the four magical elements of nature. He chuckled as he rested his back on the bark of the tree, the roughness digging into his scalp. Josh would be impressed that he even remembered what the witch had shared with them about the elements around them. The truth was, he did pay attention. Quite a bit of attention, actually. What else did he really have to do with his time? He glanced down at the laptop resting across his thighs, sighing. That's why he took Julian's offer about helping Para-Force out. If he were honest with himself, he would have to admit he had considered rejoining the team, even though he hadn't shared his thoughts with anyone else. It was the last time he truly felt like he had a purpose, and what was the point of living if you didn't have a purpose?

He glanced down at the screen, references to The Iron Dagger not even grabbing his attention at the moment. Too many thoughts of what he was missing in his life filled him. Almost everyone around him had found their mate and moved on with their lives, planning their futures and sharing everything that happened to them. They had someone to go home to, to cuddle up on the sofa with, and wake up with. He always woke up alone. He knew that there were others in Bull Creek who had yet to find their destined mate, but they were surrounded by others who were still single just like them. He was surrounded by mated couples, people who had plans to get married and have children, grow old together, and have puppies running around the yard. He was happy for them, of course, but it was also a constant reminder of what he lacked in his life, and sometimes, that was almost too much for him to bear.

He shut his laptop, tossing it to the ground beside him as a sigh slipped past his lips. *I just need to shift and allow my bear to roam, maybe do some fishing, expend some energy, get my heart pumping again.* It had been too long since his heart felt anything, really. He gained that from his team and fulfilling their missions. He felt it again when he helped save little Erin Fletcher and then helping protect the people of Bull Creek. That's who he was; someone who stepped in between others and the danger that threatened him.

Pushing himself off the ground, he stood, stripping himself of his clothes, and tossing them down on the ground with his laptop. The wind blew in off the water, caressing his flesh just before he allowed himself to shift. He howled as his bones snapped and popped, his body transforming from his human self to his giant black bear. His body thickened as fur slid out from under his skin, and he fell to his massive paws just as his hands and feet finished shifting, his arms and legs shrinking down to his thick, muscular legs. He felt his nose stretching as his forehead rose, and his ears slid to the top of his head, as his fingernails shrank and then stretched to his sharp claws. As soon as the shifting finished, he shook his massive body vigorously, stretching his muscles and getting the rest of the kinks out.

He swung back around, his senses bombarded even more than normal with the scents that surrounded him: the salt water of the creek, the cypress and pines towering around him, even the richness of the soil under his paws. His fur ruffled as the wind blew over his thick body, making his ears twitch slightly. Dropping his head in a quick, jerky motion, Ezra blew out a breath of air through his nose and then gave his body another shake.

Turning, he moved closer to the edge of the water, lapping it up as he stood there, the water splashing against his legs and soaking his dark fur. The water was cool, easing his nerves slightly as he stood there, still feeling sorry for himself. It wasn't like him to allow his melancholy to get the better of him, usually able to push through it, and force himself into a better mindset. This time, however, everything seemed like it was looming over him.

He gave his body another vigorous shake, correcting himself. He hadn't been this melancholy since he helped save Erin Fletcher, but he had pushed past it. Hell, he actually thought he was a fairly jovial guy over the past year, back to his old self. He was back on track with his life, even to the point of helping Julian and the others. So, why now? Why was all of this bothering him now?

Perhaps that's exactly why, though, he thought as he padded around in the water, looking for a fish to devour. *I'm too settled, too comfortable. With my life back on the right path, it's only shown me what else I'm missing. Everyone else has someone in their lives, and I'm left all alone, with no chance of finding my mate in Bull Creek.* He continued to fish as he continued down that line of thought. If his mate had been in their little community, he would have already found her, because he had met everyone there. His bear would have scented her the moment he saw her, as was the way of destined mates. The fact that he hadn't scented her yet meant she wasn't there, so he would need to find her somewhere else. It was true that the others found their mates because they came to Bull Creek on some mission or were sent there to help defeat someone or, as in Arlin's case, to avoid some punishment, but that was never some guarantee. He could go years or maybe even his entire life without his mate arriving. He wasn't prepared to wait that long.

A fish jumped in front of him after bumping into his leg, and Ezra's bear leaped on it, pinning it to the floor of the creek with his front paws. He turned until he faced the shore, and then with a swipe of his paw, he flung the fish up onto the grass where the creature flapped about, desperate to be back in the water. Making his way out of the creek, Ezra sighed, knowing he would be enjoying another meal alone. He was tired of being alone.

Plopping down onto the ground, he pulled the fish toward him, pinning it down with one paw as he bit into its side, ripping a chunk off and chewing. *Yeah, I'm definitely tired of eating alone,* he thought as he swallowed the raw fish.

"That doesn't look too appetizing," a voice from the past said, and a growl erupted from Ezra's bear, his lips curling up to reveal his sharp teeth, as he turned his gaze to face the man. Mattox Rumfield stepped closer into the clearing, a look of disgust on his face. "Leave it to an animal to eat like one, though, I guess."

Ezra felt every muscle tighten, as images of the past flashed through him. Tina would never let him hear the end of the fact that she warned him Mattox would find him. He should have been more careful.

Cocking his head, he stayed where he was, glancing over at the other man. He saw no point in making any sudden moves, not knowing what the other man had on him as far as weapons or whether he was even alone. *You know they're looking for you, right?* he sent to Mattox through the mindspeech of the shifters. *They'll assume you would come here. Para-Force already knows you're out and about.*

Mattox shrugged. "Assuming is not the same as knowing," he said, slipping his hands into his pockets. "Kind of reckless of you being out here all alone like this, regardless, don't you think?" He shook his head. "I guess you're not the same as you once were. Of course, I hear it happens to the best of us. Well, to you, anyway. It hasn't happened to me, which is why I was able to find you and sneak up on you. I never let my guard down." He cocked his head, turning it toward the woods behind him. "Like now, I know one of your precious new friends is walking toward us." He turned back to Mattox. "Should I kill him while you're eating? You know, like a dinner show of sorts. Your animal could feast on him, as well. Do you eat all animals or just innocent fish?"

Ezra leaped to his feet, his bear's mouth stretching as he roared, the guttural sound reverberating off the surrounding trees.

Mattox simply chuckled as he made a gun with his fingers

and acted as if he were about to shoot Ezra. "I'll be seeing you," he said. "Soon." He then turned and walked off in another direction, disappearing into the woods just as Josh emerged at a brisk run, scanning the area for danger.

"What?" Josh asked, his head still on a swivel. "What happened? What's wrong?"

Ezra sniffed the air, pointing his nose up as he tried to follow Mattox's trail. He sighed, lowering his head. It was no use. The man was gone. *It's all right*, he sent to Josh. *At least, for now.* He dropped his gaze to the remnants of his dinner, his appetite gone. With a sigh, he shifted, his bones once again popping and cracking until he stood naked at the creek's edge. When he finished, he walked over, snatching his clothes off the ground. "Someone from my past was just here," he said as he slipped his shirt over his head. "He's not someone I expected to see again."

"Who is he?" Josh asked. "What did he want?"

Ezra slipped his pants on, wishing he had thought to bring a towel with him before he went into the water. "For now, I assume he just wanted me to know he was here. Outside of that, I can only guess." He finished dressing and then turned back toward the road.

"I take it he's from one of your missions?" Josh asked as he stepped up beside Ezra, walking back toward the cabins.

"Yeah, a dark one," Ezra told his friend. "I killed his brother."

"Yeah, that'll etch your name in the man's memory, for sure. So, tell me what we're up against."

Ezra didn't even argue with his friend. He already knew there was no way he would talk his friend down from helping him or getting involved. "They were human traffickers, mainly children. It's always children. Fuckers." He shook his head, sighing. "Why is it always children?"

"What happened?"

"Para-Force was called in, and we did our job. We found where they were headed and did what we do best; we ambushed them. Mattox's brother, Jace, stood guard over a giant moving truck full of kids they were about to shove onto a shipping boat. I took him out while the others went to rescue the kids." He sighed, shaking his head as he shoved his hands into his pockets. "Jace's men killed half if not more of the people they had kidnapped before we could take them all down. Mattox slipped away in the confusion, disappearing until the other day. Tina warned me he had surfaced again, but I didn't think he would come here. Hell, I didn't think he could find me here." He sighed again. "Apparently, I was wrong."

"And what are they? Vamps? Witches? Shifters? Leprechauns?" Josh shuddered. "I hate leprechauns. Little men who could slip under your door and raid your candy jar. Pesty buggers."

Ezra rolled his eyes. "Would you be serious? Sheesh. They're gorillas."

"Gorillas?" Josh glanced at the treetops above him, a concerned look on his face. "He could be above us right now. What the hell?"

"Relax," Ezra said. "He made his point. He won't be in the trees. He wants me to sweat a little first."

Josh shook his head. "At least we had a few months of peace and quiet. Why does everything happen here?"

Ezra chuckled as they left the woods and stepped onto the gravel road. "What was it you said to me a year ago? Oh, yeah, welcome to Bull Creek."

Chapter Nine

Winnie couldn't shake Mattox's threat as she walked through the forest, doing her best to stop her shaking. She knew he meant everything he said, too, which made it even that much worse. She saw what he could do a couple of years ago, and she never wanted to see that again. Deran might think working with Mattox was worth the risk, but she knew better. When you skated close to the flames, sooner or later you're destined to fall into the fire. She didn't intend on getting burned; she just needed to figure a way out before she was engulfed in whatever the other two had planned.

The wind rustled the branches of the trees around her, pulling at her red hair as she touched the bark of the cypress as she passed it. She reached out with her senses, touching the essence of the tree as she walked on, pulling some of its power within her. She had a feeling she might need it before it was all said and done. Somehow, she needed to get away from Deran and Mattox. If she was smart, she would just turn around and run the hell away, get as far from the others as she could. Yet, something inside of her told her she needed to warn someone. After meeting Adira, Eve, and Alanna, she knew there were decent people in Bull Creek. They didn't deserve for Mattox to punish them for what whoever this Ezra was did to his brother. Hell, his brother deserved what he got, as far as she was concerned. They were trafficking humans, selling them off to the highest bidder for whatever perversions they had in mind. She barely escaped, and when she did, she got everyone else killed. She sighed as she slid out of the woods, turning onto the gravel road. These people deserve better, she thought as she turned toward the main road.

The sun dipped lower in the west, the giant cypress and pines casting lengthy shadows along the ground. Deran was stronger than her, and Mattox definitely more devious, so how she expected to overcome either of them, she had no idea, but somehow, she had to discover a way. She didn't know who this Ezra was, but somehow, she needed to find him and warn him about what was happening. If she could talk to Adira, perhaps the witch could warn Bull Creek's alpha, and together they could find a way to put an end to Mattox's plan.

Up ahead, she saw the flashing light of Everglades' neon sign, and remembered Adira mentioning how they usually hung out there. With any luck, they would be there this Thursday night, as well. Somehow, she needed to talk to someone, if only to share the burden.

As she stepped inside the paranormal bar, she paused a moment to allow her eyes to get adjusted to the dim lighting. Off to her right stood a large wooden bar with a burly man working behind it, his thick shaggy hair constantly falling into his eyes. Next to him was a smaller blonde with ample breasts and a constant smile for everyone she served.

Winnie allowed her gaze to wander around the interior, hoping to see any of the people she had already met. Even if Adira wasn't there, perhaps one of the others could point her in the right direction. Stepping further into the bar, she glanced over and noticed Deran sitting at a round table, shuffling a deck of cards. A couple of others sat around the table with him, stacks of chips in front of them as they watched him shuffle.

He glared across at her with narrowed eyes as he watched her move further into the bar, arching one of his brows as he stared at her.

She shuddered, knowing that he had a direct line to Mattox, and if she somehow slipped up in front of him, then her life would be just as over as everyone else's in Bull Creek. She sighed, trying to figure out how to get her warning out to the others without getting herself killed.

"Winnie, right?" a familiar voice said from behind her.

Turning, Winnie noticed the blonde from earlier standing there with a tall, dark-haired man beside her. Putting on her smile, Winnie nodded "That's right. How did things go after you left me earlier?"

"So, you're the one I have to blame for her constant chatting," the man standing beside the blonde said, chuckling as he shook his head. "She hasn't stopped talking about all these ideas that weren't floating around her head this morning, but now won't stop nagging at her. I think my life just became more chaotic."

Eve swatted the man's stomach playfully, shaking her head. "Please, you're just happy to have me busy again and you know it." She then introduced Winnie to the man, an Arlin Landry, and then asked if Winnie was there to meet anyone.

"Not really," she said. "Adira had told me the locals liked to hang out here, so I thought I would pop in and see what I could find." She glanced around the bar. "Seems cozy enough." Which, to Winnie, was a nice way of putting it.

Eve just giggled as she placed a hand on Winnie's arm and nodded. "It kind of grows on you," she said. Then she gestured toward the back of the bar. "Come on over and meet the rest of the gang. If you're going to be staying here a while, you might as well get to know your neighbors."

"Thanks," Winnie said and then followed the smaller woman as she made her way among the cluster of tables toward a high-top table in the back.

Several others clumped around the table already, most with beer bottles in hand or whiskey glasses. Adira held a glass of wine, Winnie noticed, smiling as she guessed at each one's personality based on the drinks in their hands. It didn't surprise her that it was the other witch with the glass of wine. The woman held an air of sophistication to her that seemed to say she preferred the nicer things in life. Weird that she was even in Bull Creek.

"Well, hello, again," Adira said, smiling over at her. "Glad you made it out. I looked for you last night, but I just assumed you were exhausted from moving into the cabin and putting everything away."

Winnie nodded. "I was, actually. Sorry. I took a hot shower and then climbed into bed for a long night's sleep."

"She gave me a reading today out at Gracie's," Eve said as she slid up to the table, shoving her hands into her pockets.

"Yeah, and now my life just became more complicated," Arlin said, sighing dramatically. He glanced over at the man beside Adira, whom Winnie assumed was the alpha of Bull

Creek. "Take my advice; don't let her do a reading for Adira. It'll cost you."

"Oh, hush, you big baby," Eve said as she swatted at the man's stomach again.

"Hey, everyone," a perky blonde said as she sidled up to the table. "What can I get you to drink?"

"Hey, Brianna," Eve said. "I'll take a Mojito, please."

"Whiskey for me," Arlin said, handing over his debit card to open a tab.

The server glanced over at Winnie, a soft smile on her lips. "And for you?"

"I'll just take a glass of Pinot Noir, please." Winnie glanced behind the server to where Deran sat, eying her as he dealt the next game. She wondered how much he had accumulated from the other men, and she didn't mean merely cash. He was skilled at prying information out of people and them not even knowing what they were sharing, because to them it appeared as idle chitchat.

"Coming up," Brianna said as she turned and walked back to the bar.

A loud noise came from the back, a group of men cheering from what Winnie could tell, followed by laughter as they ribbed someone who apparently just lost at something. She glanced around, trying to see who else was there, and if Mattox was one of the customers hiding in a dark corner. There was no one she recognized, however.

Just before she turned back to those at the table, the front door opened and a portly sheriff walked into the place, glancing around until he spotted Winnie's table.

She forced herself to remain calm as he crossed the floor to where they stood, casting a quick glance at Deran. The other man watched everything over the hand of cards he held, looking almost as if he were bored. However, Winnie knew better. Deran would have called forth his power just in case he needed to make a quick exit, something Winnie fought not to do right then. These people were simply going about their lives like they always did. No one knew there were a couple of criminals in their presence. *Breathe, Winnie.*

Turning back to the others, she heard another shout from the back, which jerked her attention in that direction.

"I hate this game!" she heard someone shout, followed by even more laughter.

A few seconds later, a small group of men stepped into the front part of the bar, laughing as a thick, brawny man patted a smaller, dark-haired man on the back. She also noticed Alanna with them, walking beside the man who seemed to be being consoled by the larger man, more than likely the loser of whatever transpired in the back room. Winnie stood there a moment, watching them as they crossed the room toward their table. Something about the larger man seemed familiar to her, but she couldn't place where she saw him before. She studied him harder as he teased the smaller man with them, and from the way it sounded, she guessed the smaller man was the one who hated whatever game they had played in the back room.

"I take it you beat his ass again," Adira asked the redhead once they reached the table.

Alanna nodded, a smug smile on her face. "I think he would much rather give me quarters for the jukebox now." She glanced over at Winnie, smiling as she reached for one of the beers in the middle of the table. "Hello, again. Did you have a good day after we left?"

Winnie glanced over at Deran one more time, noticing the way he narrowed his eyes at her. *What the hell is his problem?* "It kind of went downhill after that," she said as she turned back to the group around the table. "So, I called it quits and took a walk in the woods. Sometimes, just getting out in nature helps calm my nerves."

"I can understand that," Adira said.

"Me, too," the brawny man said as he finally looked up from his smaller friend and looked across the table at her. As he stared at her, his eyes widened a moment, his pupils dilating slightly as he sucked in a deep breath. "I, uh, I'm," he stammered as he reached across the table to shake her hand. "I'm Ezra Havlin. I haven't seen you before."

She felt her pulse quicken at the sound of his name. This was the man Mattox intended to punish. She took his strong hand in hers and shook it, still staring at him. "I'm Winnie. Winifred, really, but I prefer Winnie."

"Both sound nice to me," he told her, and suddenly, she thought he recognized her from that night a couple of years back. How would he have even seen her, though? She had been tossed into the backseat of a car, and as soon as Mattox saw Ezra kill his brother, he ordered his driver to get the hell out of there.

"Thank you," she said, softly, feeling the blush warm her cheeks. "What was the game you were all playing?"

"Um, Asteroids," he told her. "A video game Jake got yesterday." He seemed to force his gaze away from her then, as he wrapped a thick hand around his friend's neck. "This is Josh, and he gets his ass handed to him every time he plays."

"And I love being the one to do it," Alanna said, grinning as she bounced her brows at Josh.

"Hi," another man said as he reached out to shake her hand. "I'm Jake, one of the owners of this place. Welcome to Everglades."

Just then, Brianna returned with their drinks. Winnie, however, didn't notice the other woman setting them on the table, unable to take her eyes off Ezra. This powerful man was the reason she was there. The people around her table were the ones Mattox intended on hurting to make Ezra pay for killing his brother. Somehow, she needed to warn him of the danger heading his way, but how?

As she stood there, she noticed he couldn't take his eyes off her for long, constantly staring at her. He knew her; she just knew it. He recognized her from that night, and now was deciding on what he would do with her. Fear rippled through her, as she wondered if she had been foolish in wanting to help these people, after all, or if she could redeem herself before it was too late.

Chapter Ten

Ezra stood there staring at her, his bear growling within as he felt his pulse quicken. He had never seen her before, but somehow his bear wanted her, and Ezra had to tamp down on the sudden urge to take this woman into his arms and throw her down on the floor and have his way with her. Never before had he felt such a sudden rush of desire fill him as his cock started to harden in his pants.

Yet, the look on the woman's face showed more fear than anything else, and he worried he came across as some imbecile and scared her, something he knew, without even knowing why he knew it, that he would never do on purpose.

Josh nudged him in the ribs, chuckling slightly. "Forgive my friend here," Josh said. "He sometimes has trouble with the English language."

Winnie blushed slightly, a soft smile decorating her lips. Ezra wanted to kiss those lips with a hunger he never felt before. What the hell had gotten into him? His bear had never—

He stopped, his eyes widening a little. There was only one reason a shifter's animal would behave the way his bear was right then. Somehow, his animal had scented this gorgeous woman as his mate, and that scent drove the bear crazy. Hell, it would drive them both crazy until they could consummate the calling. Yet, how do you do that with someone you just met? And she was a witch, not a shifter. She wouldn't understand what his bear was putting him through right then.

Josh elbowed him again, shaking his head.

"Um, yeah, sorry," Ezra said. "I, uh, just had something random pop into my head, and it kind of threw me for a second. Welcome to Bull Creek. Have you been here long? Are you staying long?" He leaned over the table, his bear wanting to sniff her, but halfway across, he realized what was happening and yanked himself backward, his eyes going wide at the fool he was making of himself. "I'm Ezra."

"Dude, she knows," Alanna said, shaking her head as she leaned on the table. "You told her right before you went all psycho on her. You feeling all right?"

He glanced over at his friends, the ladies giving him odd looks, but the men shooting him knowing looks. They had all gone through the same thing at one point or another, so they could tell why Ezra acted like a bumbling idiot at the moment. "Yeah, I'm fine. Promise." He turned back to Winnie. What a beautiful name. "I'm sorry."

She gave him a slow nod, a curious expression on her face. "It's all right. Really. Should I repeat my name to you, as well?"

"What?" He closed his eyes, chuckling softly at the joke she made at his expense. At least she had a sense of humor. "No. No, that's fine." Opening his eyes once more, he smiled over at her. "I promise, I'm not always like this."

"No, sometimes you're worse," Alanna deadpanned as she rolled her eyes.

"Winnie here has been telling fortunes in front of Gracie's," Eve said, her perkiness drawing everyone's attention away from Ezra's awkwardness. "She does an awesome job, too. You all should get her to do a reading for you."

"A fortune teller, huh?" he asked, leaning on the table once more, smiling over at her. His bulkiness took up half the table, making the others shift slightly as he refused to budge. "That sounds fun."

His redheaded Winnie shrugged, still wearing an uncomfortable expression. "It can be good or bad, depending on how the person I'm reading for takes what I tell them. Sometimes, fortunes are hard to interpret, and we don't always see things clearly."

Her words were stiff, her tone hesitant, and he worried he had scared her too much, and that he ruined his chance to talk to her about what had really just happened. She also cast a couple of furtive glances over her shoulder at the men playing poker, which made Ezra wonder if she was already attached to someone else. God, he hoped not. That would suck. Totally suck. He wanted to get her alone. No, *needed* to get her alone, find out everything about her, where she came from, what her favorite color was, did she like turkey club sandwiches, enjoy fishing, why she was in Bull Creek. There were so many questions rambling around in his brain, it was hard to get any of them straight. How the hell had the others gone through this and not gone crazy? Hell, he had only met the woman five minutes ago, and he felt as if he was about to suffocate with the way his bear prowled around within.

"I'd love for you to do a reading on me sometime," he told her.

A snort of laughter shot from Josh's mouth as the man reached for his beer. "I can do a reading on you right now, and I bet I wouldn't be far off."

"Behave," Alanna said as she held her hand out. "Quarter. I want to play the jukebox."

"Why don't you ever have quarters of your own?" Josh asked, sighing as he dug into his front pocket for the requested coin. "What happens if I run out one day?"

"Then you have lost your usefulness," she said, winking at him.

Ezra chuckled as he shook his head, glad to have something to focus on other than the sudden desire that raged through him for the woman he just met. Turning back to her, he asked, "So, does that make you a witch, like Adira?"

Winnie nodded. "It does. Although, I kind of think we each have different skill sets and interests." She glanced over to the other witch, as if asking if she were right.

Josh and Alanna strolled off toward the jukebox, and Ezra used their absence to move closer to Winnie as he followed her gaze to see Adira nodding. "I would agree with that. Witches tend to follow different paths of interest, and I'm guessing divining is yours. Mine is more toward the elements."

Winnie nodded, her eyes sparkling as the topic of conservation turned toward something more up her alley. "It is, even though I have a keen interest in the elements, as well, and how they speak to us." She glanced over her shoulder one more time, looking at the poker table, her countenance tightening slightly.

Ezra turned his attention to where the men played poker. He

recognized Deran, who had arrived about the same time as Winnie, Ezra noticed, making him wonder if Deran was the man she kept looking at. There were also a couple of the ranchers from Blackwater Ranch to the east of them, and a vampire from Karena's clan out by the edge of Crabgrass Creek. "Do you know those people?" Ezra asked, glancing back at her, a neutral expression on his face.

She spun her gaze back to him, her eyes going wide for a moment. "What? Oh, no," she said as she took a deep breath, and he could tell the smile on her face now was forced. He could also smell the deception on her and worried she might be in some sort of trouble she didn't want him to know about. "I don't know anyone in town, having just arrived myself. I just find the game interesting. It's as much a skill as it is a game of chance."

Ezra nodded, but inside, his bear growled. Something wasn't right. He glanced back over at the men around the poker table, staring at Deran who stared at the cards in his hand. The man had sent up Ezra's red flags when they first met, and now, those flags were truly waving. Just then, Deran glanced up and locked eyes with Ezra, sending a shudder throughout the brawny man's body. Ezra turned back to Winnie, but she had already spun back around and was lost in conversation with Adira about something concerning tree roots and the sap from pine trees. *What am I missing?*

As he glanced around at the others, he noticed Dimitri staring at him, one brow cocked. Ezra simply shrugged, not sure what to tell the other man. Something was off, but he had no idea what it was just then. He wished he had his laptop. He took a deep breath, his decision made. "Tell Josh something came up," he said as he threw a twenty on the table. Pointing to the money, he added, "Use that to close my tab, will you?"

"Where's the fire" Jake asked, picking up the twenty, his

brows furrowed. "You only had one beer. This is way too much."

Ezra shrugged. "I'll get the change later. I need to get back to what I was doing for Julian. I'll be back if I can. If not, I'll see everyone tomorrow at the bonfire." He turned to leave just as he heard Winnie ask about the fire he mentioned. He chuckled as he headed for the front door. Everyone asked about Dimitri's bonfires, but truth be told, they were one of the things that brought their little community together in the beginning.

Ezra climbed into his Jeep and headed for home, doing his best to remember what the man leading the poker games said his full name was. He didn't know why he hadn't thought about checking into the man the other day. Hell, he had the resources, the people to help him track down someone who didn't seem on the up and up. Why had he failed to use them?

As soon as he reached his cabin, he slid onto the barstool around the island between the kitchen and living room, flipping his laptop open. Opening the site Julian gave him access to in his research for The Iron Dagger, Ezra typed in the name Deran Sheridan, and prayed he had remembered the man's name right. He sat there, his insides twisted into a knot as he stared at the screen. *Come on, come on. Bloody Internet.* It was one of the pitfalls of living way out in no man's land.

Finally, the page opened, and there was a picture of the man back at Everglades playing poker. Ezra scrolled through the information. Wanted for grand larceny, a scam artist, con man. He was wanted in several places for grand theft and even more for petty crimes. How the man avoided getting snagged so far, was beyond Ezra.

He continued to scroll, looking for close contacts. The news report he read said that Deran had a known associate who usually pulled the scams with him. As Ezra scrolled down to the associate's name, he froze, the mouse poised over the name.

Winifred Preston. He didn't want to click on the name, afraid it would actually be her and not just a coincidence. Sucking in a deep breath, he forced himself to click the mouse.

Another page opened, revealing his beautiful mate, Winnie. His bear growled, pacing in tight circles within Ezra. How could this be so? How could his bear scent a criminal as his mate? Something else had to be going on; he just wished he knew what it was.

He leaned back on the barstool, staring at the screen. He grew nauseated as another coincidence filled him. He clicked back to Deran's information, scrolling back down to known associates for another name, praying he wouldn't find it there. There was no way the woman his bear desired could be caught up in—

But, there it was, staring back at him. Mattox Rumfield.

Ezra felt as if his heart were breaking over the woman's betrayal, and he had just met her. It was inconceivable that he should have these emotions coursing through him. Hell, she didn't even know he had feelings for her, feelings his damn bear had suddenly shoved into him. He rarely fussed at being a shifter, but right now, he hated what was being done to him beyond his control. And if he didn't act on it, he knew eventually, the mating call would drive him crazy. He had heard the stories. They were never pretty.

He stared at the screen some more, wondering what to do about what he had learned. Should he give her a chance to explain? Perhaps it was just a coincidence that all three of them were there at the same time.

He sighed, shaking his head, knowing that was bullshit the minute the thought left his head. He needed to find out why they were there, and then he would figure out what to do about his damn bear's mating urge.

He slammed his laptop closed. *Damn, animal!*

Chapter Eleven

She knew who stood on the other side of the door even before he knocked. However, she finished pouring her tea before going over and letting him into her private sanctuary. When she did open the door finally, she didn't even have time to say hello or step out of the way before he shoved his way inside her cabin, a scowl twisting his features. "Well, please, do come in," she deadpanned as she shut the door. "Would you like some tea? Or are you simply going to start in on whatever rant you have brewing inside that skull of yours?"

He spun when he hit the middle of the living room. "Don't fuck with me," he snarled. "You knew damn well I was out there. What took you so long to answer the damn door?"

She shrugged as she walked past him, returning to the kitchen and her tea. "What made you not call to say you were coming over? You know manners tend to work both ways, Deran." She picked up her teacup, turned, and leaned back on the counter, keeping the island between the two of them. "You really should give it a try sometime."

He glared at her, and she could have sworn she saw a vein thumping on his right temple. Poor guy was about to have a conniption. "Tell me what happened last night," he demanded. "Why were you there with Ezra?"

"I wasn't there with Ezra," she told him, shrugging. "You saw me walk into the place. I was alone. I didn't even know he was there. Hell, until earlier in the day, I didn't even know who he was. And, I also know you watched him leave without me." She lifted her cup to her lips, glancing at him over the rim. "You really should let me fix you some tea. It has great calming properties you know." She took a slow sip of her tea.

"Mattox will not be pleased that you talked to Ezra last night," Deran said as he ran a hand through his dark hair. "I can't believe you were so stupid."

"How was I stupid?" Winnie felt herself bristle as she glared at the man, holding her teacup with the fingers of both hands. "Look you dragged me out here, telling me we needed information on the residents of this little community, without even telling me why or what information I was to collect. I assumed it was because you wanted to pull some long con on them. You never told me the holder of your leash called the shots or even that there was a deeper game in play. Don't blame me if things don't go the way you want. You should have been straight with me from the beginning. Besides, Ezra joined us. I couldn't simply walk away without it looking strange, now could I?"

He shoved his fists onto his hips as he stared around at her place. "This is a cluster fuck."

"I don't see how," she said. "We talked for maybe a minute, two at the most, and then he rushed off." She shrugged. "Who knows what the man thinks? Just tell Mattox to cool his horses."

Deran scoffed. "You tell him. I prefer my hide left intact, thanks." He sighed, and then moved over to the island, sliding onto one of the stools surrounding it. "I think I'll take some of that tea."

She nodded as she turned, setting her teacup on the counter to fix him some of his own. "Have you even talked to Mattox? Do you know what his game plan is?"

"He intends on destroying this town," Deran said, clasping his hands together in front of him. "He says it's the only way to truly punish Ezra." He shook his head. "I have no idea how he intends on doing it or even when. He just wanted us to gather as much information on the people here as we can, mainly those closest to this Ezra person, and then he promised the land to me when he was finished. What he plans on using that information for, I have no idea."

Once she fixed his tea, she turned, walking over, and placing the cup in front of him. "You know it won't be easy," she said. "This entire town is made up of paranormals: shifters, witches, even vampires. Mattox is one gorilla. How do you think he's going to destroy an entire town?"

Deran shook his head. "I have no idea, to be honest, but have you ever known the man to fail when he set out to do something. If he says he'll destroy the town, then I believe him."

She nodded, walking back to grab her cup once more. As she turned back around, she asked, "How did the poker game go?"

He shrugged. "Good. Met a couple of hands from the ranch east of here. Blackwater ranch, I think, was the name of it. They seemed friendly enough. The vamp was a little cold, and not just because of the lack of blood running through his body. He seemed distant, aloof. I almost wondered if he was a plant at one time, but then, he never won a hand, so who knows."

"Did the sheriff stop and talk to you?" she asked, leaning back on the counter.

He shook his head. "No. Just walked in, did a short circuit of the joint, and then left as quietly as he entered. Who knows what he wanted? Probably just a routine check."

"And did you find out anything about why we're here or about the people who live here?"

"About the same as you," he told her. "There's supposedly a bonfire tonight. I think you should go. I'll stick to my poker game at that disgusting bar. If you can get into some of these people's heads, we may be able to figure out how to—"

Someone knocked on Winnie's door, cutting Deran off. Both of them jerked their gazes to the door, confusion as to anyone else visiting her on both their faces. Winnie closed her eyes a moment, searching with her senses to see—

Her eyes popped open as she jerked her attention to Deran. "It's Ezra," she whispered.

He cocked a brow at her. "What the hell is he doing here?"

"How do I know? He acted all weird last night as if something had touched him in the head." She motioned toward the back of the cabin. "Go out the back way."

"Winnie, are you here?" Ezra called out, knocking on her door once more.

"Be right there," she said as Deran moved to the hallway. He paused once he reached it, and Winnie grabbed his teacup to stow it out of sight. Rolling her eyes, she waved him on. She didn't need his suspicions right then. She had enough to worry about as it was.

A minute later, she opened the door to see Ezra standing

there, his strong hands shoved into his pockets, and a timid expression crossing his face. If she had to guess, she would swear it was an expression he didn't wear often. "Ezra," she said, smiling. "What brings you by?"

He glanced over her shoulder as if he expected to see someone there, and then she wondered about what she had heard concerning the strength of shifter hearing. Had he heard her talking to Deran? Looking back at her, he sighed as he bounced from foot-to-foot, his brows furrowed. "Well, first, I wanted to apologize for my behavior last night. I'm not normally that befuddled." He shrugged, his expression shifting into a more playful, boyish look. "My animal sometimes throws things at me that make me stumble a little. Last night was one of those times."

She smiled as she opened the door wider. "There's nothing to be sorry about. I can't imagine it would be easy living with two personalities in one body." She stepped to the side, motioning to the inside of her cabin. "Did you want to come in for a moment?"

He gave a slow shake of his head. "Maybe after I say the other reason I came here," he told her, a troubled expression washing over him. The man had more facial expressions than anyone she met before. "You might not want me in after that."

"That sounds kind of ominous," she told him, crossing her arms over her chest as she stood on her threshold. Had she read him wrong?

He ran a hand through his dark hair again. "Well, Bull Creek doesn't get a lot of visitors as you can imagine, and we've had three just this week alone. The guy you noticed playing poker last night came by the bar earlier in the week, and something about him just seemed off to me. Well, when I saw him last night, and I saw how you kept looking at his table—"

Winnie sighed, dropping her gaze to her feet. "You put two and two together and came up with us working together at some point in the past."

"Well, not at first, to be honest," he told her. "I left in a hurry last night because I wanted to run his name through my database with Para-Force. They're an organization I work for on occasion. It was then that I saw you were known associates and had even run some of your scams on people together."

She nodded, glancing back up into Ezra's dark green eyes. She felt her heart beat faster as she stared over at the giant of a man, his broad shoulders and powerful chest aching to have her head lay on them. "And so you thought the two of us were here together to pull another con." She needed to think fast. Deran could still be around listening in on their conversation, and as much as she wished she could tell Ezra the truth right then, there was no way she would risk anyone getting hurt, especially him, until she figured a way out of this mess. "Actually, I was just as surprised as you when I saw him. He and I split a while ago." She made a soft sigh as she dipped her head again. "That's not my life anymore. I didn't want to be the reason people lost their money, and well, I kind of disappeared on him. Shocked the hell out of me when I saw him sitting there last night. That's probably why you saw me cast a quick glance over there all the time. You just never know what Deran is up to these days. Plus, I didn't want him stirring up trouble for me here. As I said, I'm not that person anymore, and I didn't want it to taint the friendships I'm starting to collect here in Bull Creek. I'm beginning to like these people." She felt her smile growing. "Even the befuddled ones."

He nodded, his lips pressed together in a thin line as he glanced back out at the trees alongside her cabin. Somehow, she could tell there was something else he wanted to say, and that Deran wasn't the worst of it. She stood there, waiting for him to screw up the courage to simply ask her what he wanted to ask.

Blowing out a breath, he shook his head and glanced up at

her, a pained expression on his face. Somehow, she needed to keep a list of how many ways the man looked at her. "As I glanced through Deran's known associates, another name popped up. One from my past that, oddly enough, had come across my attention again."

Winnie had a sinking feeling in the pit of her stomach, afraid she already knew the name that would slip from his lips.

"Mattox Rumfield."

She bit back a groan, knowing full well there was no way she hid the shock on her face from him. She should have known that a man with his connections would have access to everything, including criminal records. He would have already discovered her connection to Rumfield, as well. She swallowed, gliding her tongue between her lips to moisten them. Her heart pounded, and she could feel it in her ears as she stared out at Ezra. She didn't know what to say, so she just stood there, saying nothing.

Ezra nodded, his lips still pressed into that thin line of his. "I can see the name rings a bell with you, too." He sighed as he turned and walked back to the steps leading back down to the ground, his hands still in his pockets as he stared out at her gravel driveway. He didn't seem angry, or suspicious. He just seemed hurt, somehow, and she had no idea why. They had only met last night. They barely spoke. Why was he taking her past as some personal attack?

"I don't know how much you know about shifters," he said, still staring out at the road in front of her house. "We don't get to choose our mates, like normal people choose a spouse."

She stared at his back, still unsure of what he was talking about.

He glanced up at the sky. "The reason I acted so weird last night was because my bear had finally scented his mate, the lady he wants to spend the rest of his life with." He turned so that he stood sideways, able to look at her without really facing her. "Last night, he scented you. He wants you as his mate." He laughed, brittle and choppy. "And you're connected to the man whose brother I killed a couple of years ago an who now wants to hurt me somehow. You're a criminal, and I don't know what to do with that." He stared at her for another moment and then turned and walked away, his shoulders slumped, gaze fixed on the ground in front of him. Defeated. If she were to choose a word to describe him right then, that would be it. Defeated.

Tears filled her eyes, and she had no idea why. Why would she cry over this man she just met? Then, as she stood there, she asked herself how she couldn't cry for him? The universe had aligned their paths, and her past slammed a roadblock between them. And he still didn't know that Mattox intended on killing him.

Chapter Twelve

Ezra threw another log onto the fire, flames sparking and shooting into the dark sky above as the wood rolled until it finally settled against another log. Shoving his hands into his pockets, he stood there, staring into the crackling flames as they danced, reaching upward in the hopes of breaking free and spreading. He stood, mesmerized by the flames, as his mind drifted back to his conversation with Winnie. She denied being in Bull Creek because of Deran or Mattox, but thanks to his animal, he could tell she was lying. He just didn't know why. He had also heard her talking to Deran inside her cabin just before he knocked on the door.

He sighed. *Yes, I do. Why would she admit being associated with two hardened criminals?* Somehow, he needed to figure out why they were all there. Whatever it was, it couldn't be good.

"What's up with you?" Josh asked as he and Dimitri stepped up beside Ezra. "You seem even more pensive than normal."

Ezra glanced over at the smaller man, his brows furrowed. "When am I ever pensive? I'm the happy one around here."

Josh shook his head. "Not lately. Over the past few days, maybe the past two weeks, you've seemed more melancholy than jovial. I had hoped you digging back in with your old unit would help you snap out of it, but if anything, it seems to have dragged you deeper into your funk. So, what's going on in that thick head of yours?"

Ezra turned his focus back to the fire, debating within whether or not he should tell them what was going on. Of course, so far, there wasn't anything happening, but with Mattox, that would change in time. He took a deep breath. He didn't have the right to keep this to himself. They needed to prepare for whatever was happening so no one got hurt. There were too many innocent people in Bull Creek. Yet, if he did, they would know his mate was in on whatever was about to happen. He needed time to protect her, even though she wasn't there to protect him.

He glanced around, scanning the others at the bonfire, hoping Winnie would have made an appearance. He saw Nathan Landry and Ash Merickle, Lainie and Rance, Eve and Arlin, even Karena, the vampire who ruled the coven of vamps out at the edge of the small community. There were others, as well, but not his Winnie. It would have been so much easier if she were there to explain things to him before he had to tell Dimitri about Mattox, but in good conscience, he couldn't risk others getting hurt because of his own personal issues.

He sighed, shaking his head. "Mattox Rumfield is here," he told the others. "I also looked up the guy who's running poker games out of Everglades, and he's dirty."

"You did a background search on one of our people?" Dimitri asked as Josh asked, "The guy from yesterday you told me about?"

Ezra nodded at Josh. "Yes, him," and then he turned to Dimitri, "And Deran Sheridan isn't one of our people. He doesn't stay in Bull Creek; he just scams our people." He turned back to Dimitri, shaking his head. "I'm afraid Mattox is someone from my time with Para-Force. I thought he had vanished, died even, but it seems I was wrong. He's here, and he intends to hurt me somehow."

"Have you called Chet?" Dimitri asked, crossing his arms over his chest as he turned and faced Ezra. "And why did you wait so long to tell me? What if he went after you while you were around others, like last night at the bar?"

Ezra didn't look at him, keeping his gaze fixed on the blaze in front of him. "I haven't told anyone, not even Josh really. Tyra warned me that he was out, but I was arrogant enough to think I was beyond his reach." He shook his head. "It's just like before. I thought I was untouchable, but some bad guy comes along and proves me wrong. Even my damn bear screws with me."

"Your bear?" Josh asked, his head tilted to the side a little. "What's wrong with your bear?"

Ezra simply shook his head. "A long story." He wasn't ready to tell them about Winnie just yet. They knew enough to help him prepare for an encounter with Mattox. They didn't need to know that his bear scented his mate, and she turned out to be one of the ones sent to hurt him.

Dimitri motioned for Lainie to join them as he asked, "Did your background search dig up any outstanding warrants?" He turned his attention back to Ezra, and the look on the alpha's face told Ezra the man was definitely not happy with him. He couldn't blame Dimitri. His silence could very well have put people in danger.

"He's wanted in several places, including St. Augustine, which he just left," Ezra said, still staring at the flames. He needed a focal point right now, something to keep his anger from getting the best of him.

"Who's wanted in St. Augustine?" Lainie asked as she and Rance joined them. "Wanted for what?"

"Grand larceny," Ezra replied. "He steals from people."

"Who does?" Rance asked, confusion on his face. "And why are we talking about it here in Bull Creek if it happened in St. Augustine?"

"Because apparently, he's at Everglades setting up poker games," Dimitri said, his tone clipped, full of anger. "He's also teamed up with one of Ezra's former criminals, who just so happens to be here to kill him. Or, at least, that's what I'm assuming you mean by 'hurt'."

Ezra felt Lainie and Rance turn their gazes toward him.

"Someone is here to kill you?" Lainie asked. "When did this happen?"

"It hasn't happened yet," Ezra said, sighing. "But he arrived yesterday. Or, at least, he made himself known to me yesterday. I don't know how long he's been here."

"And you didn't say anything to any of us?" Rance asked as Lainie pulled her cell phone from her back pocket.

"We've gone through that already," Josh said, and Ezra could feel the empathy in the man's voice.

"Chet, we need to send someone to Everglades," Lainie said as she stepped off to the side and away from everyone else. "There's a man there hosting a poker game..." Her voice trailed off as she walked further away.

"Why does this man want to kill you?" Rance asked, his tone

a little less stressed.

Ezra glanced over at the man, wishing he had better answers. "Because I killed his brother when we went after them for human trafficking." Of course, it hadn't been the last time Ezra had seen Mattox.

"We've been here for two hours," Kacey Carmichael snarled. "This fucker isn't showing up."

"All the chatter I've heard says the opposite," Benny said as he leaned back on the ground, his hands clasped together in his lap, eyes closed. "He'll show up. He has interests here."

Kacey growled at the coyote shifter, her wolf threatening to come out and trash the man.

"Calm down, Kacey," Julian said in their ears. "We need to take Mattox down, and this is all we have for now."

"Easy for you to say," Kacey snapped. "You're back at HQ all warm and cozy, while we're out here trying not to get drenched in this fucking storm."

"It's not dark enough for me to travel, and you know it," Julian said, calmly. "I need you to keep your control."

Ezra glanced over at the wolf shifter, knowing calm was about the last thing Kacey ever was. The woman was constantly set on volatile. He glanced around the warehouse, keeping his eyes peeled for any sign of movement. Liam had shifted into his capuchin monkey and scurried around the roofs, while Colton huddled in a dark corner on the other side of the warehouse, already in his gorilla form. Ezra had kept from shifting for the moment, deciding it best to have a few of them on two feet just in case.

He grew tired of listening to the others bitch at each other, their impatience getting the better of them. He glanced over at Benny, stretched out on the ground. Okay, only Kacey was impatient. Still, her mood swings could get a little much at times.

"I'm going to go look around," he said as he turned and walked off along the edge of the warehouse, keeping to the shadows. He seemed to always be in the shadows.

With his shifter hearing, he could hear Liam scurrying about, could hear Colton breathing on the other side of the warehouse, could hear—

He stopped as a sound reached him that didn't belong. A ticking noise. No. Four ticking noises. He spun, trying to focus on the noises to determine where they came from. "Does anyone else hear that?" he asked, knowing the others could hear him thanks to Millificent's magical earbuds. Having a witch on the team came in handy at times.

"Hear what?" Liam's voice came through the earbuds, another part of Millificent's magic. The earbuds would shift with them, fitting in their animal's ears just as well as their human forms.

"There's a ticking, like a bomb," Ezra said, reaching into his back pocket for his flashlight. "Several bombs, actually." He flipped his flashlight on, shooting the beam around the place, no longer worried about being careful.

"What do you have?" Julian asked.

Ezra could hear the others in motion now, saw other beams of light as the rest of Para-Force stood and started their own search grid. He continued to search, having no information to give Julian. Shooting his beam of light up at the ceiling, he noticed Liam hopping over a hole in the roof. Off to the side, Colton's gorilla came out of the shadows, his fists dragging the ground, his head on a swivel as he searched for the noise.

"Found one," Benny shouted, his flashlight illuminating a dark box on the ground with a timer.

"Found another," Kacey shouted in another corner. "Who the fuck sets bombs to go off when they don't know anyone will

be here? There has to be something here he's trying to hide."

"Get out of there," Julian cried out in their ears. "It's a trap. Damn it, its a trap! You're the ones he's trying to—"

Ezra spun, but just as he did, the first explosion sounded, ripping the air and slamming him to the ground, the air whooshing out of his lungs. The other bombs went off, one after another. He heard the rest of his team screaming, heard the screech of Liam's monkey as it fell from the collapsing ceiling. Ringing sounded in his ears, drowning out the rest of the screams from his teammates. He rolled over, every muscle in his body screaming at him. He could feel something trickling down his face and into his eyes, blood more than likely. He tried to sit up, but pain screeched through him. Wiping the blood from his eyes, he tried to open them, to see where the others were, but all he saw was the face of Mattox Rumfield as he stood on the edge of the building, half the wall gone as flames engulfed the rest.

The man stared at him, using his fingers like a gun and pulling the fake trigger.

Ezra just stared at him. Message received.

"Everyone had been pretty battered," he told the others around the fire. "Liam broke a leg, and Colton broke his collarbone. Kacey and Benny were scratched up, but otherwise all right. I had a concussion, but my anger kept me from passing out." He glanced over at Dimitri. "He could have killed us then, but had counted on the bombs taking us out for what we did to his brother and the others of his team. They were monsters. When we took his brother down, before his men could be apprehended, they murdered most of the people they had kidnapped. We took half the Rumfield crime ring down, but lost most of their victims. Mattox made it clear he would get his revenge, but then he simply disappeared. No matter what we did or Benny's Underworld connections, we couldn't find him.

Eventually, we moved on, thinking him either dead or out of the country." He shook his head, turning his gaze back to the flames. "Seems he merely bided his time, just like back then. The man stood there, watching us waiting for him until I got up and started moving around. I drew my teammates into that shit storm. Me."

"It wasn't your fault," Josh told him. "You were doing your job."

Ezra shook his head. "My job almost cost me my team."

"Your silence could have cost you some of us," Dimitri said, anger still masking his face. "We do things together here. Just like you did in Para-Force. Never forget that again."

Ezra gave him a curt nod, wishing he knew whether or not he did the right thing back then or even right now. With his bear scenting Winnie as his mate, he began to doubt his own decisions.

"Chet's on his way to Everglades," Lainie said as she rejoined them. "He's calling Wes to give him a heads up, and Johnson is with him."

"He's a male witch," Ezra said, turning back to Dimitri. "Chet will be out of his element if Deran decides to fight. So will Wes and the others."

"Then I guess we better get there, hadn't we?" Dimitri said, his gaze locked onto Ezra's. "We do this together."

"Together," Ezra agreed, determination filling him. This was his team now. He needed to trust them just as he trusted Para-Force.

Chapter Thirteen

Winnie walked toward the bonfire, still not sure what to do with what Ezra told her at her cabin earlier. She had heard shifters chose their spouses in weird ways, but never imagined it would be because of the animal inside of them. She wanted to talk to him about it, explain more about her actions, that she didn't want to do what the others were forcing her do, but by the time she reached the bonfire, she noticed Ezra walking off with some of the others. None of them looked happy.

"Party ending early?" she asked Eve as she approached the roaring blaze.

Eve shook her head, laughing softly. "Just another day in Bull

Creek. From what I could make out, there's some wanted man at Everglades running a poker game. They're on their way to help the sheriff out. Apparently, the man is a male witch, so they don't think the sheriff can handle it without their help."

A knot twisted in Winnie's stomach, and she forced herself not to react. They were going after Deran. Ezra was going after Deran. There was no way he would go quietly, and she knew it. He'd use his magic to trash the place, making his escape during the chaos. More people would get hurt. Innocent people.

She fought the urge to race out of there, knowing how that would look. Still, she wanted to get to that bar, see if she could help the others in some way. Her nerves tightened, and she had to tamp down on her anxiety as it made her hands tremble slightly. She took slow, steadying breaths as she reached out to the elements around her, pulling from the fire, the trees, the nearby creek, and even the air surrounding her. She called them to her, power that she knew she would need if she went to the bar.

Yet, what would she do if she *did* go? Could she stand against Deran for the benefit of the others? What would he do if he escaped? And she knew he would escape. There was no way the others could take him down, even with all of their powers and strength. Deran was just that damn good.

As she stood there, Eve chattering away about something Winnie didn't even hear or really cared about, all she could do was think about the mess Ezra would be walking into when he confronted Deran. Surely, however, Ezra knew what the man was capable of, having been a part of that special forces group before. And then it dawned on her that Ezra was here in Bull Creek and not off somewhere fighting bad guys. Did that mean he had left the team? And why settle here in such a quiet, backwoods town?

As soon as she had as much power as she could hold from the elements, she excused herself, telling Eve she was tired from talking to so many people throughout the day. "I really am sorry," she said. "Sometimes telling fortunes takes a toll on me, and if I don't get my rest and rejuvenate my depleted resources, I can barely move the next day."

Eve nodded as if she understood. "I get it, trust me. You have to do what's best for you. I appreciate what you did for me earlier. It really helped answer some questions."

"I'm glad," Winnie assured her and then moved off toward her cabin, just so Eve wouldn't know she had other plans.

Just as soon as she was out of sight, however, she deviated and headed for Everglades, cutting a path through the woods like she did earlier. She wished she had thought to get her own car before allowing Deran to drag her out in the middle of nowhere, but it was too late to worry about it now.

Night cast everything in shadows, and the moon barely penetrated the thick branches overhead. Normally, Winnie would have used her magic to light a path, but she didn't want to use up her store of power in case she needed it when she reached the bar. She had to trust that her senses were good enough to get her safely through the woods.

By the time she finally did arrive, the others had already disappeared inside. Two sheriff's cars were parked in haphazard fashion in front of the bar, their blue lights spinning in the darkness. She stopped, staring at the structure for a moment to determine if something was happening, but so far, everything looked quiet.

With a deep breath, she started once more toward the front of the bar, but just as she was about to reach it, the wooden door blew outward, and the one she knew as Josh was thrown into the parking lot. He tumbled over, rolling a few times before coming to a stop, his body a crumbled mess.

Right behind him, others poured out of the bar, some

screaming, others just running for their lives. Some tripped over their own feet or those of the others escaping with them, but no one stopped to help them up.

The sight of Josh lying there spurred Winnie into motion, her magic at her fingertips as she squatted down to see if Josh was all right.

He groaned, one hand going to his forehead. "Someone catch the license plate of that bus?" he asked, clenching his eyes shut as he simply laid there.

"Are you all right?" she asked, using her magic to scan him for more serious injuries.

He nodded as he sat up, propping himself up by his elbows. "Yeah, I'll be fine. One thing about shifters is we heal quicker than humans."

She nodded as she shoved herself back to her feet, and turned toward the door. "Good."

"Wait," Josh cried after her. "Don't go in there."

But she had no choice. She would not allow Deran to hurt these people.

As she stepped through the shattered door, she stopped to take stock of what was happening inside. Deran had his back against a wall, his hands sparking red fire from his magic, and in her gut, she knew he had performed a blood ritual before coming there that evening. She continued searching the interior, looking for Ezra. Tables and chairs were overturned, some splintered into thousands of pieces, and one sheriff sprawled along the floor, unmoving, while another, an older man, portly with shaggy gray hair, stood, gun drawn as he stared at Deran. Some of the others had shifted into their animals, and Winnie noticed a wolf and a Florida panther hissing and growling at the male witch. Adira stood in front of Deran, her arms down at her sides as the blue flames of her magic swirled around her hands. Other people huddled behind overturned tables or under pool tables, and in the middle of the room stood Ezra, still in his human form as he glared at Deran.

The male witch turned as he saw her step into the bar, her eyes wide with shock at what she saw. Ezra also turned to look at her, and she saw the questions on his pained expression. Was she there to hurt him, as well? She knew he wondered if she would stand with Deran or stay out of it. And by the way Deran stood straighter, a smug expression covering his face, the male witch assumed she was there to back him. He was sadly mistaken, she thought, as she stepped further into the bar.

Deran turned back to the others as Jake came out of the back where the pool tables were, and Wes moved out from behind the bar. "Will you knock this shit off?" Jake demanded as he stepped closer to Adira. "We just finished putting this place back together. Why can't you people ever fight outside?"

Deran cackled as he shrugged. "I think you should have used better materials." He turned to Ezra. "You know I can end this quickly. Why not just let me go and save yourself some headache?"

"You're not going anywhere," the older sheriff said. "I have a warrant for your arrest, and from what I could tell, there are several cities fighting to see who gets you into their court systems first. I'm going to enjoy handing you over."

Deran sneered as he lifted his hand, red magic sparking around his fingertips. "You won't be handing me over to anyone," he snarled as he shoved his arm outward, magic ripping from his hands, and shooting toward the sheriff.

Adira yelled as she threw up a barrier between the older man and Deran's power. Both magics collided, sending Adira flying backward to land on a tabletop, shattering it as she crashed to the floor.

The panther shifted, revealing Dimitri standing there in the nude as he screamed out Adira's name, racing to where she rolled over on the floor.

"More furniture?" Jake groaned. Then he tightened his fists, growling as he shifted, his dark brown bear coming out of his clothes, snarling and snapping its fangs as he moved toward the magician.

Deran just laughed as he raised his arms again, only this time, before he could shoot his magic bolts at the bear, Ezra stepped in between them, his eyes narrowed and his muscles taut. Deran lashed out, flinging his red magic from his fingertips toward Ezra's chest. Ezra didn't even attempt to move out of the way.

Winnie screamed as she flung her hands up, throwing her own magic out of her palms as she called on the elements. Power ripped from her as she sent a bolt of magic to intercept Deran's blast and then, before anyone had time to react, sent another sizzling shot across the air to hit Deran in the side, sending him flying toward the bar.

Ezra jerked his attention toward her, his brows furrowed in question, but Winnie didn't have time to answer him. Deran would not be down for long, and she needed to act before he could regain his senses. She had taken him by surprise once. She wouldn't manage to do it a second time.

"I need her," she shouted to Dimitri as she pointed to Adira. "Now!" She gathered more power into herself as she took a deep breath, filling her lungs with as much air as she could hold.

Dimitri helped Adira to her feet, and the other witch stood, wobbling slightly, but her magic already at her fingertips as she held onto her mate for support.

Josh entered the bar again just as the wolf flung itself at Deran, who had started to haul himself to his feet. The bear followed the wolf, both prepared to pin him down if they could.

Wes grabbed a whiskey bottle, holding it like a club as he rushed to aid the others.

"No!" Deran roared as he flung the others off him, bodies flying in all directions as he stood to his feet.

Winnie shoved another bolt of magic at the man, hitting him from the right as Adira hit him with her magic from the left. He simply laughed, sneering at them as he raised his arms higher, ready to lash out with his power.

Winnie could feel her power growing weaker, could tell that Adira was still feeling groggy from where he had flung her across the bar. They wouldn't make it. He was still stronger than both of them. If he sent another bolt of his power at them, especially Adira who had already been hit once, he would kill them. She sucked in a deep breath, calling on all of her reserves, and flung one more bolt of magic at him, the power hitting him and sizzling into the air as it burned his clothing.

He just stood there, laughing at her attempt. "I do believe it's my turn now," he snarled as he lifted his hands. He turned to Winnie, sneering as he took a step forward. "You never should have betrayed me." Red magic swirled around his hands as he gathered his power to him.

Winnie braced for whatever was about to happen.

However, just as he prepared to shove his magic at her, she watched as his head made a sudden forward jerking movement, and then he collapsed to the floor. Behind him stood Wes, the bottle still clutched in his hand.

The brawny man stared at the bottle, his lips pressed together. "Interesting," he said. "In the movies, the bottles always break."

Josh chuckled as he walked over and slid onto one of the barstools, a hand to his head. "Thank god it didn't. Maybe that bastard will stay out for a while."

"Any idea how we keep him from using his magic when he

does wake up?" the sheriff asked, running a thick hand through his shaggy hair.

"I have a better question," Dimitri said, reaching to the floor and grabbing what was left of his shirt. When he stood back up, he turned to Winnie, one brow cocked. "What did he mean about you betraying him?" He then turned to Ezra. "And did you know she was in on this?"

Winnie glanced over at Ezra, pain etched on his face.

He simply nodded as he glanced across the bar at her. "I did," he said. "But I couldn't exactly give her up. I needed to figure out something first."

"And just what was that?" Dimitri said, his voice almost a growl. "More secrets. Damn it, Ezra, look what happened here tonight because you didn't warn us. What was so fucking important that you couldn't tell us everything?"

Ezra kept staring at Winnie, and her heart broke for what his friend was putting him through. He took a deep breath, and then said, "She's my mate."

Everyone just stood there, staring at him.

Chapter Fourteen

He knew they were pissed, but there wasn't anything he would have done differently. Winnie Preston was his mate, and he had to protect her, even if she had been sent there to kill him.

"Do you want to run that by me again?" Dimitri asked. "She's your mate? When did you find this out?"

Ezra shrugged as he started across the room toward the redheaded witch. "Last night, actually, when I suddenly was at a loss for words. My bear scented her, and then everything else came to light." He shook his head. "I didn't know about any of this until late last night."

Josh looked at Dmitri, shrugging. "We all kind of guessed it with the way he behaved when he saw her. It just wasn't confirmed."

"Wait," Jake said as Noel handed him some clothes she had brought out of their office. "You knew these bastards were here and didn't warn us?" He jerked his hand around at the shattered furniture. "Do you see what they did to our place? Why the hell would you keep this a secret?"

Dimitri stood there, arms over his chest as he glared at Ezra, and all Ezra wanted to do was walk over and take Winnie in his arms and hold her tight. He knew they were all mad at him, and they had a right, if he were honest with himself. He should have told them, but he just needed time to figure things out. "I didn't think they would start a magical fight in your bar," Ezra said.

"How could you not—" Jake started, but Josh cut him off.

"We brought this to your bar," he said. "Not Ezra." He glanced over at Lainie and Dimitri, then at Ezra. "While it's true he should have warned us a little bit sooner, you two made the decision to come after the witch while he was here." He pointed to Lainie and Dimitri as he spoke. "We should have waited until he left. Caught him outside after hours when no one else was around." He placed his hands on his hips as he looked around at the mess scattered everywhere. "We're all to blame for this bullshit, not just Ezra." He then glanced over at Winnie, sighing before he turned to Alanna, a soft smile toying at his lips. "And we all know what we would do to protect our mates. I won't hold that against him, either."

Ezra smiled over at his friend, nodding his appreciation for what Josh said.

Jake slipped into his clothes, his movements clipped, full of pent-up rage. "You people need to figure your shit out faster before you bring it to our bar." He reached down and grabbed an overturned chair, setting it back on its legs. With a shake of his head, he moved behind the bar and then slipped into the office behind it, leaving the chaos behind.

Noel gave an apologetic smile to the others with a slight shrug. "I'm sorry. He'll cool off in a little bit. You know he doesn't mean what he said."

Dimitri just nodded.

Ezra watched as Noel walked over to Wes, sliding an arm around his waist, and then moving to the office where Jake disappeared, the burly man setting the whiskey bottle on the bar as he passed. "I'm telling you, I really thought the bottle would shatter once I hit him with it," Wes said as he allowed his mate to lead him out of the main bar.

Josh was right, but that didn't make the damage to Everglades any easier to swallow. The bar had seen its fair share of catastrophes just as Bull Creek's residents had. Sooner or later, this town needed to break free of the bullshit that seemed to flood into it. For a haven, it sure did possess a lot of chaos.

"Again, I ask, how do we keep him from using his magic once he wakes up," Chet asked, now standing over Deran's motionless body. "Somehow, I don't think handcuffs will work."

"I can help with that," Winnie said as she crossed the bar, moving to where Deran lay sprawled on the floor.

Ezra watched, worried that the male witch would wake up and attack her now that she stood against him. However, Deran remained unconscious as Winnie squatted down, placing a palm on the man's forehead and closing her eyes. With a deep breath, she started chanting words Ezra couldn't make out. A slight buzz rippled through the air of magic being spent, and then Winnie settled back on her heels, her palms resting on her thighs. She glanced up at Dimitri and then the sheriff. "I put a sleeping spell on him. He'll be out until I, or someone of equal power, wakes him."

Dimitri glanced over at Ezra. "I think this is something Para-Force needs to handle. Local law enforcement isn't equipped for a male witch in their custody."

Ezra nodded once. "I'll give Julian a call and have him send someone out here to pick up Deran."

"Good," Dimitri said, and then he turned to Winnie, taking a deep breath as he slipped his arms over his chest. "Now, do you mind telling me what he meant when he said you betrayed him?"

Winnie stood back to her feet, and Ezra could see her hands trembling. He wished he could make the others trust her, but so far, only his bear had sensed the good in her. Still, she was his mate, and he wouldn't let her face things on her own.

Walking across the bar, he took her hand in his, and squeezed it. "It's all right," he assured her. "We just need to know the truth of everything. Can you do that?"

She glanced up into his eyes and nodded. "I'm sorry I wasn't completely upfront with you before."

He kept holding her hand as he walked her over to one of the tables, reaching down, and setting it back on its legs. He then reached for a chair as everyone else helped set the furniture that hadn't been destroyed back into place, some of them sliding down into the chairs to catch their breaths. Gesturing for Winnie to take one of the empty chairs, he slid into one beside her, and then took her hand in his again, hoping to give her the reassurance she needed. "Now, tell us what happened?"

Winnie smiled over at him and then turned to Dimitri, who remained standing, arms over his chest as he studied her, obviously not caring that he was still naked. Ezra knew it was something the witch would have to get accustomed to if he were to keep her in Bull Creek once all of this was over. "Deran and I have been partners for a couple of years," she said. "And not by my choice, I assure you." She then told them of how she tried to rescue the people Mattox and his brother had kidnapped and intended on selling, how Mattox spared her, even though they killed most of the others, saying he wanted to use her powers. She spent the next couple of years forced to help Deran scam people from town to town, every once in a while having to do a job for Mattox that required her special skills. He left her alone for the most part, but when he snapped his fingers, he expected her to jump. "I didn't know he was a part of this when Deran told me we were coming here. All I knew was that we were to gather information about the place and its residents, get to know you, and find out everything we could. He would do it through his poker games and me through my fortune telling." She glanced over at Ezra. "It wasn't until I was here that he told me about Mattox and what Mattox intended to do."

"Kill Ezra," Dimitri said.

Winnie shook her head. "No, that's not it. He intends to kill the rest of you, instead of Ezra. He promised your town to Deran to use as a place for his coven if he helped gather the information he needed to determine who was closest to you." She turned her gaze to Ezra. "He wants to make you hurt by hurting everyone else around you, and leaving you alive."

Dimitri glanced up at Ezra, his eyes narrowed in his anger. "That would have been nice to know ahead of time. We wouldn't just be collateral damage in this fight. We're the damn targets."

Ezra simply sat there, staring over at Dimitri, not knowing what to say to what he just heard.

Dimitri stared at the giant man for another moment and then turned to Winnie once more. "Do you know where Mattox is now?"

She shook her head. "Deran demanded to stay out at that motel on the highway, saying he needed to keep space between you and him in case things went south. He put me in the cabin to make me look more open to people. I've only seen Mattox once when he visited me yesterday in front of Gracie's. He threatened to hurt me if I didn't do as he said."

"I take it there are warrants out for your arrest, as well?" Chet asked her as he stood from where he just handcuffed Deran.

She shrugged. "I honestly don't know. I've been associated with Deran for two years, so I'm sure there's been some connections made."

Ezra squeezed her hand. "We'll figure it out." He turned to Dimitri, a knot twisting in his stomach. "We can't allow anything to happen to her. I won't let Mattox get his hands on her."

Dimitri sat there, staring at him for a moment, when Adira walked up behind Dimitri, placing her hands on his shoulders. "We're not going to let anything happen to her," she assured Ezra. "We just need to figure out our next move. If the whole town is in danger, then we need to do everything we can to protect it." She turned to Winnie, a soft smile on her lips. "And everyone in it, including you."

Chet shook his head as he turned. "I never saw her," he said as he walked over to his fallen sheriff, the younger man stirring and turning into a sitting position.

Ezra watched as the old man helped Johnson to his feet, the taller man holding his head. He then glanced over at Lainie. "Help me get him to Doc Henderson. He can give him a looksie and see if I need to take him to the hospital in Melbourne. Then we can haul this dipshit into my car so I can take him to the department." He glanced over at Ezra. "That's where I'll keep him until your team can make arrangements to get him." He then glanced at Winnie, smiling. "It was a pleasure not meeting you." He dipped his head and then helped Johnson to the front door, Lainie swooping in and holding the wounded sheriff up on his other side.

Ezra watched as they slipped through the door and out of sight before turning back to the others at the table. Shame colored his cheeks as he took each one in. These people had always stood by him no matter what, even when they had no clue as to who he really was. He should have trusted them from the very beginning. "I'm sorry," he said, glancing directly at Dimitri. "I should have spoken up sooner. I honestly didn't know what to do."

Dimitri locked gazes with him for a moment and then gave a curt nod. "We'll figure it out," he said. He turned to Winnie. "I suggest you take her back to your cabin. If Mattox gets wind that she stood with us against Deran, he could go after her." He then turned to Winnie. "I also think you need to keep to your routine as much as possible. Be at your table telling fortune's tomorrow. Hopefully, Mattox will see you and think you don't know what happened." He glanced around at the others then as he leaned back in his chair. "I think we need to scout around the woods and see what we can pick up. I'll reach out to Karena and have her help out at night. Mattox will need to be close to carryout his plan. We just have to find him."

"I'll check the old airport," Josh said. "Those warehouses would make a good hideout."

"We'll check the airport," Alanna said. "We should make sure none of us are alone if he plans on going after us, instead of Ezra. Safety in numbers."

"What kind of paranormal is this Mattox?" Rance asked, his hands planted firmly on his hips.

"A gorilla shifter," Ezra answered. "And a strong one. He and his brother were almost unstoppable."

"Until they were," Winnie said. "I watched you take Jace down. Your team almost caught them all."

Ezra sighed. "And look how many people were killed when

we did." He shook his head. "No, I won't take him for granted." He glanced over at Dimitri. "He's dangerous. Alanna's right; none of us should be alone."

"I guess I can make new wards," Adira said. "We don't have any gorilla shifters in Bull Creek, so I'll just make it to ward against those."

"I would like to help," Winnie said. "This is just as much my mess as anyone else's. Let me help fix it." She glanced at Dimitri, her expression pleading. "Please."

Dimitri looked at Ezra. "My gut wants to say no, but if your bear thinks she's your mate, then I have to trust him. Our animals wouldn't lead us astray."

"Are you kidding?" Alanna scoffed. "Look what mine stuck me with."

"Watch it," Josh said. "Or you'll lose your quarter supply."

"You say such sweet things," the redhead said as she leaned into Josh's side, kissing his cheek.

Ezra smiled at them and then turned to Winnie, his hand still in hers as a soft smile toyed at his lips. He now had someone to share his quarters with.

Chapter Fifteen

Winnie felt her nerves tighten as she opened her cabin door, Ezra standing behind her. He had refused to leave her side for even a minute, insisting on following her to her cabin to get what she needed to stay at his place. However, she still thought it was a bad idea.

"Ezra, Mattox is here for you," she told him. "What do you think will happen when he discovers I'm not where I need to be, and instead, I'm at your place? It might stir things up faster. We need time to locate him before he causes trouble and hurts people."

"There's no way I'm leaving you here alone," Ezra told her, determination on his face. "We don't know yet whether or not he knows you stood with us at Everglades, or if he knows about Deran's capture. How far does his reach go? What if you two weren't the only ones he brought in on his plan?" He shook his head, planting his fists on his hips. "Nope. Not going to leave you here alone."

She crossed the room, placing a hand in the middle of his chest. "Then don't leave me here alone," she told him, her voice soft as she glanced up into his eyes. "Stay here with me."

He glanced at her, a smile creasing his face. "I can do that. I know we just met, and there's still so many questions between us, so many things that need explained."

She nodded, as she stared up at him. "I'm sure. As you said, we still have some things to discuss."

He stared down into her eyes, his own eyes a dark chocolate brown that melted her panties with the passion that resided behind them. He was brawny, with powerful shoulders and thick arms, shoulders you could sit a coffee cup on without worrying about it toppling over, and hands she could imagine gripping her and pressing her to him as he ravaged her mouth with his own. Her honey dripped just thinking about it. Yet, he had a gentleness about him that warmed her heart, making her feel safer than she ever had before.

With a quick nod, he motioned for her to sit down on the sofa.

She did as he asked, sitting there with her legs together, turning slightly so she angled more toward him than facing outward. "I need to apologize," she said, beginning the first of her confessions. "I lied to you earlier when I denied being a part of Deran's plans here. Well, I wasn't exactly a willing participant." She told him about their first day here about three days ago and how she told Deran that the residents of Bull Creek deserved to be left alone, that they had seen enough pain to last a lifetime. "I hoped I could figure out how to stop him before I had to tell you about my part in his plans." She shook her head. "I should have known better than to try to outwit a shifter and one who worked for Para-Force to boot." She smiled over at him, placing her hand on his. "I was there that night, you know. I saw you rush toward Jace once he left the truck, your bear attacking him and dragging him out to the high grass." She then told him once more about how Mattox had kept her in his car, and even when the driver wanted to turn around to help Jace and the others, Mattox told him to flee.

"The man always had a knack for saving his own ass," Ezra said, a sadness to his eyes now. "I'm sorry you had to see that."

"I'm not," she told him. "It's what helped me realize I needed to help you somehow now. I don't want to be bound to this lunatic anymore. I want free of him, just like I'm now free of Deran."

"You know once Mattox finds out Deran's been captured, he's going to come after all of us," Ezra said. "He'll come after you just as hard as he's coming for me. We need to keep you safe."

"I'm pretty good at protecting myself," she assured him. "I've survived his world this long."

"Well, as far as I'm concerned, you're never going back there again," he told her, a stern vehemence in his tone that made her smile. "Tell me you don't want to keep living like you are."

She smiled at him, squeezing his hand. "I don't. I promise. I never did, to be honest. It was thrust upon me, and I was weak enough to think I couldn't escape, even though the cards told me differently. I gave myself a reading a few days before coming here, and the cards told me to expect change. I just didn't think it meant this much change." She titled her head to the side. "Have you ever had a reading?"

He shook his head. "Nope. Never."

She nodded as she patted her thighs just before standing. "Hold on, and I'll get my cards. If you're going to stay here tonight, then we have all the time we need to see what's in your future."

When she returned, she handed the cards to him, telling him to shuffle them for as long as he wanted. "This will get your thoughts and essence onto the cards. Think about something you want to know about as you shuffle."

She watched as he did as she told him, shuffling them in several different ways before handing them back to her.

"We'll do a three-card spread for now," she said as she straightened the cards.

Sliding the first one from the top, she said, "Nine of Swords." On the card was a dragon surrounded by swords. She pressed her lips into a thin line. "This represents your past and speaks of your isolation." She glanced up at him, wondering about what the card revealed. Every time she had seen him, he had been surrounded by people, but that didn't mean he never felt alone. "You need to open yourself up some, look for new ways to communicate and interact with others."

He nodded as he stared at the card, his face unreadable.

"This next card represents your present situation," she said as she flipped over another card. "The High Priestess." The card held the High Priestess standing between two pillars which represented secret knowledge and initiation. "She's the guardian of things hidden. What she's telling you is to trust your gut." She smiled as she looked up at him. "You always know what's best for you."

He nodded once more, smiling this time as he looked over at her. "It's hard when it involves people you care about."

She smiled, reaching over and placing her hand on his wrist. "I understand that. But from what I've seen of you, your gut doesn't steer you wrong. You found out about Deran and me because you followed it, right?"

He smiled, giving one curt nod. "True."

She turned back to the spread on the table. "Now, this last card is your future." She flipped it over, laying it beside the others. "Eight of Cups." On the card was a dragon above a river that appeared unending. "The water is indicative of our emotions. The full moon you see symbolizes the high tide of the river, representing the ebb and flow of the water in connection with the full moon." She glanced up at him, her brows furrowed. "This tells me you're looking for something on a much deeper level than what you have right now." She set the rest of the cards on the table and slid back in her seat. "Does this show you anything about yourself?"

Ezra stared at the cards, his lips pressed into a thin line.

She didn't press him, allowing him the time he needed to process the information she gave him.

Finally, he sighed as he leaned back on the sofa. "Well, to be honest, I have isolated myself a lot over the past couple of years due to something that had happened while I was on Para-Force." He glanced over at her, his expression soft, almost forlorn. "I thought I was getting past that when suddenly I glanced around and all of my friends had found their mates." He made a sheepish shrug. "I guess I started feeling like I was alone again, but this time for a different reason."

"Their mates," she repeated. She took a deep breath, staring at him as one question burned in her mind. "You said your bear scented me as his mate. How is that possible? You just met me?"

He shrugged. "That's just part of the curse of being a shifter," he told her. "The animals inside of us get to pick and choose who we are destined to be with for the rest of our lives, and if we ignore their choice, we run the risk of going insane. Very few have been able to refuse the mating call and survive."

"So, if we don't... What? Get married or something? Then you're going to go bonkers?" She had heard tales about something like this but never truly believed it was true. How horrible not to have a say in who you spent your life with.

He chuckled. "Some would say I'm already bonkers, but yes, that's pretty much the gist of it." He placed his hand on top of hers, sandwiching her hand between his muscular palms, and Winnie sucked in a breath as the sensations of his touch rippled through her. "But, I'm not going to force you into anything. I'll do whatever I can to protect you, always, but I won't force the mating call on you."

She smiled over at him, tilting her head slightly as she stared into his eyes. "And what if I said you weren't forcing me?"

He stared back at her, his brows furrowed in confusion, a dumbfounded look on his face. "You mean..." She watched as he took a slow breath. "But you just mentioned how we just met. And yet, you'd still want to... With me... I mean, it's not like..."

She laughed, his stammering making her fall for him even more. "I know, it's crazy, but then again, isn't the mating call supposed to be crazy? I know we just met, and I know we've got a lot to figure out, especially with Mattox here breathing down our necks, but," she took a deep breath before continuing, "I know this is what I want. That you are who I want. I'm ready to be crazy with you."

He slid his hand up to her cheek, cupping the side of her face as he gazed deeply into her eyes. "I know it's too soon to say the big L word, but god, Winnie, you are so much under my skin in all the right ways. I'll be honest; I suffered from some fairly large bouts of depression and loneliness before you arrived. I was ready to leave Bull Creek and join the team again."

She reached up, placing her hand on his as he pressed it

against her cheek. "I'm glad you didn't, or I never would have found you. And I think you're the one I needed in my life all this time."

He nodded, and then she felt him pull her head toward him, bouncing his gaze between her lips and her eyes until he kissed her, hard, his breath warm against her cheek.

She groaned as she surrendered to the kiss, falling into him as they sat there, lost in whatever they were at the moment. She didn't even know, if she were honest. All she knew was that she needed this man in her life, and she would do anything to keep him safe.

When they broke the kiss, she leaned back, staring up at him as the reality of their situation flooded back in on her. "I still think we should stay here tonight. If Mattox hasn't caught wind of what happened at the bar, then he'll definitely know something is up if I'm not here. I can always deny knowing where Deran is, but I can't explain why I slept somewhere else."

Ezra looked at her his brows pinched, and she could tell his wheels were turning.

"What are you thinking?" she asked.

"I think we should get a story out there circulating among the residents that explains what happened," he said, glancing back at her. "People love to gossip, so Mattox is sure to hear the scuttlebutt at some point."

She nodded slowly, thinking over his idea. "We spread a story along the lines of Deran was called out for cheating by someone, a vampire, or tiger shifter, or something, and that a fight ensued, which ended by someone calling the sheriff and Deran's arrest."

Ezra nodded. "It might work. But what if someone says they saw you there? How do we explain that?"

She shrugged. "The witch could be Adira, and people were confused. I could simply tell Mattox that I arrived too late to help and didn't want to risk my cover by getting involved. He'd buy it, more than likely. Knowing how much he wants the information I'm supposed to gather for him."

"It's worth a shot," he said, blowing out a breath. "It's the best we got, anyway."

"So, you're staying here tonight."

He nodded. "Looks that way. Let me call Dimitri and get the story started." He touched her nose with the tip of his finger, swiping down playfully. "You're a smart cookie, Winifred Preston. This might just work."

She watched as he rose from the sofa, pulling his cell phone from his back pocket as he did. As he walked over to the kitchen island, dialing his friend, she sat there and watched him. His firm ass, powerful legs, his soft eyes. He looked like he could tear apart a mountain but was still soft enough to pick his way through a field of dandelions without disturbing a one of them. He had a big heart, full of loyalty and protection for those he cared about. She was lucky to be one of those people.

As soon as he made the arrangements with Dimitri, he ended the call and slid his phone onto the Formica top of the counter. Grinning, he walked over to her, reaching out for her hand. When she placed her fingers into his palm, he lifted her from the sofa, pulling her closer to him. "Well, since you want me to stay here tonight, we should discuss the sleeping arrangements."

"Oh?" she said, leaning back as she stared up into his eyes. "Do you think they need discussing?"

He grinned, shaking his head. "Not at all." He leaned down, wrapping her in his powerful arms and picking her up off the floor. As he held her, he kissed her passionately, slipping his tongue past her lips and into her mouth, tasting her, claiming her.

She moaned as she swung her arms around his neck, returning his kiss with a hunger that burned between her thighs. She could feel his hardness pressing against her, and even with the chaos swirling around them, she knew this was exactly what she needed right then. *He* was the one she needed right then.

When he broke the kiss, he leaned back, grinning at her as he continued to hold her in his arms. "Do you know the great thing about these cabins?" he asked as he turned and carried her toward the hallway.

"What's that?" she asked, giggling as he refused to put her down.

"They're all built the same," he told her. "So, I know exactly where to take you." He winked at her, and the heat flamed even more deeply in her passion.

"Good, then you don't need to really see," she told him just before she leaned in and kissed him again, holding on tighter to him as she dangled in his arms. God, she couldn't wait to get back to her room. This was one fortune she hadn't seen coming her way, but she was definitely ready to claim it.

Chapter Sixteen

Any luck?" Ezra asked as he stared out at the warehouses surrounding the abandoned airport. They discovered the area a few months ago when Dimitri's father tried to sell off Fitz's ex-girlfriend to some undesirables. Luckily, they were able to stop him in time, but sadly, it ended in Fitz killing his father.

Josh shook his head. "Nothing so far. Alanna will be here in a moment, and we can get a closer look. She took time off work to help us get this settled." He glanced over at the bigger man. "I'm surprised you left Winnie alone, to be honest. Where did you stow her?"

Ezra chuckled. "She's with Adira working on those wards.

Once they get them finished, they'll spread them around the edges of Bull Creek.."

Josh nodded, his hands on his hips as he stood there, staring out at the dank warehouses. "I truly didn't expect to ever be back out here again. This place gives me the creeps."

Ezra nodded. "I get it. Who knows what history is here? What ghosts linger among the buildings? However, I think it would be a great location for a Halloween party. We should think about that. For a town of spooky people, we don't do a lot to celebrate that holiday in particular."

"What's to celebrate?" Josh asked. "We have actual vampires living out by the creek. Why would we dress up like one?"

"I don't know," Ezra said, not willing to give up his idea. "I think it would be fun."

"It would be silly," Josh said. "And the vamps would probably be insulted."

"Like the way they are when you call them vamps?" Ezra smirked as he shot his friend a quick glance.

"They can't have everything," Josh said shrugging as they heard noises coming from behind them.

Ezra took a quick sniff of the air and recognized Alanna's scent approaching. A few seconds later, the dark gray wolf appeared from around one of the cypress trees, sniffing the air as she drew closer to them.

"Anything?" Josh asked, turning as Alanna reached him, and dropping a hand to one of her ears, giving her a hard scratching.

Nothing that I could detect, she sent back with the mindspeech of the shifters. *But that's up here. Who knows what we'll find once we get down there?*

Josh turned and stared at the warehouse. "Yeah, that's what scares me." He scratched her behind her ears a little harder. "Where did you stash your clothes?"

They're in a backpack by a tree just behind us, she sent. *I figured I'd go ahead and shift before meeting up with you.*

Ezra stared at the buildings, flashbacks filling his mind of the last time his team went to a building just like these to snatch Mattox. The team took some hard hits that day, and the man still escaped. Ezra took a deep breath as he scanned the buildings. "Mattox is a sneaky bastard," he told them, before launching into his tale of what happened that dreadful night a couple of years ago. When he finished his story, he glanced at the others. "He's patient and meticulous. The man waited for over two hours to trigger those bombs. He wanted me in motion, wanted us separated, and stood there and watched until he got us exactly where he wanted us. Only then did he detonate the bombs. Luckily for us, he didn't count on our strong hearing, which was funny since he's a shifter, as well." With a slow nod, he reached another conclusion he had never considered before "Unless he did count on our hearing, making us come into the warehouse even more before realizing what was happening. Damn. And we fell for it."

Josh nodded as he moved his hand from Alanna's head. "Then we need to move slowly and carefully." With a slow nod, he started to strip as they had discussed before arriving. Ezra would remain as he was, and Alanna and Josh would shift into their animals and search that way, their stronger sense of smell and hearing gaining even more strength in their animal forms.

Once Josh finished shifting into his Florida panther, he and Alanna made their way down to the hot concrete, sniffing the ground as they went. Ezra stood there for a moment, watching them, concern etching his features. Mattox had set his team up once before. What if he was doing the same thing now? Surely, the man had some sort of escape plan, just like last time.

With a deep breath that did nothing to settle his nerves, he started down the slope toward the airport and its plethora of empty buildings. He just hoped they were actually empty.

They scouted through a few buildings, seeing nothing but dust that hadn't been disturbed in years if not decades outside of the one where Dimitri's father died. No one could detect any strange scents that didn't belong there, nor did they hear any noises out of the ordinary. The place was as deserted as it appeared.

Well, I'd like to say this was a wasted trip, but at least we know he's not here, Josh said as he sat down on his back haunches, his tongue lolling as he panted.

Ezra scanned the buildings, an uneasy feeling filling him. "I don't know," he said, as he slipped his hands to his hips. "I thought for sure this would be where we would find him. It doesn't make sense. Where the hell is he hiding?"

Are you serious? Alanna asked. *Our entire community is a hideout of sorts. There are plenty of places here for someone to keep themselves from being seen. How long did you live in that tent before Josh stumbled on you? And if it hadn't been for Miles trying to kill Lainie, we probably never would have found you.*

He nodded, knowing she was right. The warehouses would have been a perfect statement made from Mattox to them, bringing them back to the past. Ezra found it hard to believe the man had simply ignored these buildings. "Something just doesn't feel right."

What doesn't feel right is my feet on this scalding concrete, Josh said as he bounced back and forth on his paws and spun in a quick circle. *Let's get back to the woods and out of the sun.*

I agree with that, Alanna said.

However, Ezra remained where he was, squinting as he studied the tops of the buildings. The hairs on the back of his neck stood on-end as his breathing slowed, the turning of his head barely noticeable as he did what he did best. Hunted. And then he saw it, a flicker of brightness, like a light flashing on and off. A reflection of the sun.

"Get down!" he yelled, but it was too late. He heard the shot a mere second before the bullet struck Josh's panther in the shoulder, spinning the animal around and to the ground where he simply laid flat.

Josh! Alanna screamed as she raced to the panther's side, but Ezra darted over to her before she could reach her mate, snatched her up off the ground, and dove for some barrels that lined the edge of one of the buildings. A shot ricocheted off the concrete, barely missing Alanna's left flank.

"Stay down," Ezra hissed, holding the wolf in place with one hand as he glanced back over at Josh for a quick moment. The panther simply laid there, blood seeping out of the gunshot wound and onto the hot concrete. "Son of a bitch." Ezra turned to where he spotted the flash of light, now knowing it was a sniper. Mattox.

We need to get to Josh, Alanna snarled. *We can't just leave him out there.*

"I know," Ezra snapped. "But we're not going to do him any good if we get ourselves shot trying to save him, either. We need to think smart here." He sighed, feeling the icy grip around his heart. He had led his friends into another fucking trap. He should have known the warehouses would have been too poetic for Mattox to ignore.

And just what do you expect us to do? Stay huddled here forever? This isn't doing anyone any good, especially Josh.

Ezra said nothing as he stared at where he saw the bright flash of light. Would Mattox stay there, waiting for them to make a move, or would he just leave them there, counting on their fear to keep them pinned down, guaranteeing Josh's death. He glanced over at his friend. If he wasn't dead already.

Josh, can you hear me? Alanna asked, her wolf struggling to escape Ezra's grip. *Don't you fucking die on me, you son of a bitch. We haven't finished this yet.*

Still nothing.

Ezra growled. Fuck, fuck, fuck. There was no way he would sit there while his friend bled out on the concrete. He glanced around, searching for anything that would help him get to Josh. He let go of Alanna, turned, and plopped back on the barrels as he tried to think, fear and anger and concern fighting for control of his mind right then. This was worse than if it had happened during one of his Para-Force ops. Those people knew what to expect, knew the risks. Josh was a civilian. He didn't deserve this.

Then his eyes went wide as he remembered what Winnie had said. "Alanna, I need you to promise me you'll stay right here. Don't move from behind these barrels. Promise me!"

I'll do my best, she told him, and he knew it was the most she could guarantee.

He gave a curt nod. "I'm going to get Josh."

How? The minute you stick your nose out there, Mattox will shoot it off.

"I don't think so," he said. "Trust me." He turned back around, first moving to his knees, and then to his feet. He didn't hold his hands up in surrender, but rather, placed them on top of the barrel in front of him and stood there for a moment, waiting to see if he was right.

He's not shooting, Alanna noticed. *Why isn't he shooting? Do you think he's gone?* She started to rise, but Ezra told her to stop, shoving her back down below the barrel.

"He doesn't want me dead," Ezra said. "Just my friends. He won't shoot me." He glanced down at her, giving her a weak shrug. "At least, I hope he won't shoot me."

With a deep breath, he stood straighter, turned, and started walking toward Josh's panther. *You better not be dead. Please, god, don't be dead.*

Once he reached Josh, Ezra knelt down beside him, putting his body between Mattox and the panther. Running his hand over the tawny coat of the animal, Ezra tried to feel for a pulse, and then he heard the animal breathing. Slow and steady, but it was there. "Good, boy," he whispered. "Just keep playing dead a few more minutes."

He reached down, sliding his arms underneath the panther, and then lifting the animal as he stood back to his feet. Josh simply hung limp in his arms as Ezra turned and walked back to where Alanna waited.

The wolf stared at them as they approached, but Ezra said nothing. Then Alanna turned her muzzle up to the sky and howled, the sound baleful and full of agony.

Ezra's heart broke at the sound, but he kept walking toward her. So far, he had been right about Mattox's intentions. He hoped he was right for a few minutes more.

As soon as he reached the barrels, he moved to the door in the warehouse. He walked inside and set Josh's body on the ground. Returning to the barrels, he toppled them over onto their sides so that they provided a trail to the open doorway where Alanna could slither her way across the concrete and into the safety of the building.

Once inside, Alanna padded over to where Josh lay, nuzzling his shoulder with her dark nose. *How bad are you?*

I feel like I'm on fire, he told her. *Sorry I didn't answer you. I wasn't sure if he would pick up on our communication or not and finish the job.* He lifted his head slightly and glanced at Ezra. *What made you do something so stupid as to come out there and get me? He could have killed you.*

Ezra shook his head. "He doesn't want me dead. Just you guys. I knew I would be safe, which is how we're going to defeat him."

And just how is that? Josh asked, laying his head back down on the cold concrete.

"I'm going after the bastard alone."

Josh sighed. "I knew you were going to say that. Can we at least get me to Doc's first? I kind of have a couple of holes in me."

Chapter Seventeen

H ow are the people at the bar?" Winnie asked as she pulled her hot tea closer. "Do you think they're still mad at Ezra?"

Adira shook her head. "No, I don't. People around here tend to get over things quickly. You kind of have to when you depend on each other so much for your safety."

"Good," Winnie said as she lifted the cup to her lips. "Ezra's a good man. I couldn't bear it if someone thought ill of him."

Adira glanced over at her as she finished setting the stones on the table. "You seem to have grown fairly attached to him in such a short amount of time. You sure you're not part shifter?" She giggled as she smiled over at the other woman, and Winnie felt the blush warm her cheeks.

"I guess it does seem a little weird, doesn't it?" she asked, not sure how to explain the sudden attraction to the man she had only met three days ago. "Is this what happened between you and Dimitri? He's a shifter, as well, so I imagine it was sort of the same, right?"

Adira chuckled as she shook her head. "No. I mean, yes, he's a shifter, but no, that's not how it was between us. At least, not on my end. When I first met Dimitri, I thought he was an arrogant, misogynistic ass. He was always barking about how he had to protect me, and here I was the one sent to help him fight Bane. I refused to be protected like some weak female." She paused, leaning on the table with her forearms. "Do you know I even woke up one morning to his panther sleeping on my front porch?" She shook her head, laughing. "I about ripped him a new one that morning." A soft smile slipped across her face as she sat there, and Winnie knew the other witch was looking into the past, remembering the hardships that drew them deeper into each other's arms. "Of course, then things, well, they just happened, and the next thing I knew my magic was back to normal, and I had his bite mark on my shoulder."

Winnie felt her brow arch. "Bite mark?"

Adira nodded, laughing slightly as she reached up and pulled her shirt away from her shoulder. Winnie glanced at the flesh, and sure enough, there was the faded scar of sharp fangs in the woman's shoulders. "It's part of the mating process. It's how it's consummated, actually. At the point of climax, the shifter's teeth shift into the teeth of his animal, and he—or she—bites down, the magic of the shifters flowing into their mate." She reached for another stone. "That magic turned Eve into a tiger, fixed my magic, and turned Noel into a bear. Of course, Noel had two bite marks." She shook her head. "I hadn't even heard that was possible until her."

"Noel? That's the lady that owns part of the bar?" Winnie asked. "She's mated to two men?" She giggled. "Lucky woman. Usually it's the men who stack up the ladies. Of course, she'll never get the toilet seat down in that house."

Adira laughed as she finished spreading out the stones. "I'm sure they make up for it in other ways."

Winnie didn't doubt it.

They worked for another hour, Adira casting her spell over the stones to warn her if Mattox—or rather any gorilla shifter—stepped into Bull Creek. Winnie paid close attention, storing up the information for a later date. She was always on the lookout for new things, spells, herb magic, old lore she could pull from. She would add them all to her grimoire and hopefully pass it on to her daughter when she had one.

"I think that about does it," Adira said as she set the last stone in a wicker basket. She glanced over at Winnie. "You want to help me set them out?"

"You'd trust me to know where the wards are after everything you know about me?" Winnie asked, still baffled that she wasn't behind bars yet.

Adira nodded. "Why not? You said you wanted to help end this, right?"

Winnie nodded, her heart swelling a little at the thought that these people did trust her, at least enough to allow her to help them and prove herself. "Yes, I would. I'd love to see this all the way through."

"Good," Adira said as she picked the basket up off the ground. "Then let's get started."

Winnie followed the other witch as she headed for the front door, leaving her cup of tea sitting there. However, when Adira opened the door, a man stood there, blocking her way.

"Well, what a surprise. Hello, Winifred."

Winnie's eyes went wide as she glanced over Adira's shoulder to see Mattox standing there, sneering at her. She felt her eyes go wide as she backed up a step. How had he found her? And even more worrisome, why was he there?

The stones in the basket started glowing, and Adira jerked her gaze around, glancing at Winnie. However, whatever the other witch saw in her face must have told her the man on the porch was not on their side.

Adira jumped back, shoving her arm out as a blast of magic ripped from her palm and hit Mattox in the chest, picking him up off the ground and hurling him backward to land on the gravel drive, tumbling over and over, his arms and legs flailing. She backed up, not even bothering to turn around as she allowed the stone wards to fall to the porch. Slamming the door behind her, she spun, glancing around the place for something to use as a weapon. "I take it that's Mattox" she said, still searching her cabin.

Winnie stood there dumbfounded. "It is. How did he know I was here?"

"I don't think he did," Adira said, pointing toward the hallway. "Let's get out of here." She moved, leading the way. "He said 'What a nice surprise,' so I kind of think he's here for me. You did say he's going after Ezra's friends, right?" She continued down the hallway to the back door, rushing to escape the fiend at the front of the house.

"Shit," Winnie hissed. "This isn't good."

Adira shoved the back door open, but as she did, a dark blur swung down from the roof to slam into Adira's chest, shoving her back into the house and into Winnie. She screamed, both ladies tumbling to the floor.

As Winnie lifted her head, trying to extricate herself out from the other witch, she glanced up and saw a massive gorilla drop from the roof to stand in the open doorway. He leaned back, his arms out at his sides as he clenched his fists together, looked up at the ceiling and roared, saliva dripping from his sharp teeth.

Winnie felt her eyes go wide as she started to crabwalk backward, doing her best to get the hell out of there.

Adira lifted her head, groaning, and then she noticed the gorilla and threw her arm up.

Before she could send a magic bolt toward him, however, Mattox reached out and snatched at her, pulling her toward him, and then slammed her into the wall. A sharp crack could be heard as her head hit the wood, and then Mattox shoved her down to the floor, stepping on her arm as he passed her on his way toward Winnie.

Winnie stood there, clenching her fists as she felt the anger mix with her fear. "You son of a bitch!" She jerked her arm out, opening her hand as blue power shot from her palm toward the gorilla.

He ducked, growling as he lumbered toward her. *Funny that I find you here helping the witch. What were those stones? Let me guess. They were wards to warn her that I was here, right?* His mocking laughter filled her ears as she backed slowly away from him, praying Adira was all right. The other witch huddled on the floor, not moving, and Winnie worried about how hard the other woman's head hit the wall before crumbling. *I think you both were a little too late, don't you?* He kept moving toward her, bent over as he used his front hands as legs. He cocked his head to the side, studying her. *I went looking for Deran, but he's suddenly vanished into thin air. You wouldn't know anything about that, would you?*

Winnie backed up another step. "I haven't seen him since the other day when he showed up at my cabin," she lied, hoping

Mattox didn't know any different. She'd find out quick enough if he did. "And Adira and I were just working on some spells. That's all. I was supposed to get close to them, remember? She's a witch, as well." She stepped back out into the living room, hoping Adira woke up soon.

As he followed her into the front room, he swiveled his massive head, taking in the rest of his surroundings. *And yet, she slammed the door in my face when she saw me.* He turned his angry gaze back to Winnie. *I wonder why she did that if she didn't know who I was.* He cocked his head a little more as he glared at her, his mouth parted slightly, revealing his sharp teeth. He then sniffed the air, a snarl twisting his lips. *You reek of him. His scent is all over you.* A roar ripped from him as he moved closer to her in two hops. *You fucked the man who killed my brother!*

Fear coursed through her as she stumbled backward, fighting to maintain her control so she could get the hell out of there. "Ezra was just doing his job," she said, no longer seeing the need to keep up the pretense. "You and your brother were monsters. Hell, you still are. You abandoned your brother to his fate, instead of going back to help him." She reached out, calling forth the power around her, even though she doubted she could defeat the animal in front of her. She would damn well put up one hell of a fight.

He chuckled, and it ground in her head like boulders falling on each other. *So, you did get too close to these people. What happened to Deran?*

"He's in jail," she told him. "Ezra ran a background check on him and found out he had warrants. He also knows I'm involved with him, as well as you. Deran is in a cell waiting for Para-Force to get him and haul his ass away." Her heart pounded in her chest as she stood there, waiting for the attack she knew was coming her way. "They're all on to you." She stood straighter, taking in a deep breath. "They won't let you get away with what you have planned."

They won't be able to stop me. They're already wounded, emotionally wrapped up in their failures to protect their own. Ezra already feels the burden of his guilt. Now, it's time to make him feel the true weight of his crime. He growled once more and then leaped into the air, his arms outstretched toward her.

Winnie threw her arms up, blue bolts of magic shooting from her palms to strike at the giant gorilla. Her magic hit him in the shoulder, turning him slightly and pushing him back, which only made him angrier. He roared again, reaching down to the coffee table, and hurling it against the far wall and out of his way.

Winnie shoved another bolt of power at him as she backed up, but she tripped over something on the floor and the shot went wide, smashing into the wall, splintering the wood in all directions. She hit the floor hard, the air rushing from her lungs as her head hit the wood, sending bright white spots exploding across her vision.

She tried to scramble to her feet, but Mattox was too fast. He loomed over her, spit falling from his snarling mouth, and she froze, her eyes going wide in terror as she felt her entire body tremble.

Now, Ezra will know pain. And then Mattox backhanded her, her head jerking to the side as pain shot through her face. It was the last thing she remembered.

Chapter Eighteen

That hurts," Josh yelled, and Ezra could see his friend's body tighten as the pain shot through him. While the healing of shifters was quick, it still took some time to be complete. The pain would linger for a while.

Once they reached Doc Henderson's place, Josh had shifted back to his human form, having remained as his panther to make it easier for Ezra to carry him. Alanna shifted back, slipped into her clothes which she had stored nearby in the woods, and called Dimitri to tell him what happened. The alpha of Bull Creek told her he'd meet them at Doc's and then she raced to catch up to Ezra, Josh whining about how he was being manhandled by the larger man.

Ezra said nothing as he raced to the doctor's, blaming himself for allowing another person he cared about to get hurt by Mattox. He should have known the man would have contingencies for someone stumbling upon his hideout. Hell, the last time Ezra had a run-in with him, the man waited over two hours before blowing the building in on them. He would have had no problem waiting in a sniper's lair for however long it took for them to stumble upon the airport and then take them out.

As soon as they reached Doc Henderson's place, Josh shifted, and the doctor started working on the wound. Luckily, the bullet went clear through Josh's shoulder, missing anything major. That part surprised Ezra, knowing Mattox could have killed his friend easily if he had wanted.

Dimitri, Rance, and Lainie arrived moments later, followed by the sheriff, Chet Einstein, and Deputy Johnson, all wanting a recounting of what happened.

"I think we need to go out there and look around," Rance said, his arms over his chest as he cradled his elbows with his hands. "If we can see his nest, it might tell us more about him."

"What's there to know?" Josh asked as he winced in pain again, sucking in a sharp breath through clenched teeth. "Damn, Doc. Is that a rusty needle or something? That hurts like hell."

Doc kept staring at the wound he was stitching closed, his brows raised as he concentrated. "No. Why did you want me to use one?" He shook his head. "I swear, you're about as whiny as that bartender was when I fixed him up a while ago. You should have dodged faster. Then I wouldn't be doing this now, and you wouldn't be whining."

"Should have..?" Josh jerked his gaze over his shoulder to glare at the doctor, his brows pinched. "How the hell was I supposed to know I was about to be shot?"

"What good is that shifter hearing of yours if you don't use it?" the doctor asked, still staring at the wound as he slipped the needle back into Josh's flesh.

Josh groaned as the doctor continued to stitch him up. "I'm fast, Doc, but not that fast."

"I saw a reflection off in the distance just before I heard the shot," Ezra said. "But there still wasn't time to avoid it."

"Off in the distance?" Dimitri asked. "Do you remember where?"

Ezra nodded. "Almost to the end of the runway where the planes come in. I'm guessing he had something built to elevate him so he could see us."

Dimitri glanced over at Rance and Lainie. "We need to see what we can find out there. Maybe there's something there that will give us a clue as to where he is."

Lainie nodded. "Don't worry. If there is, we'll find it." She turned to leave, but Dimitri stopped her by calling out her name. She turned back around, and by the look on her face, Ezra knew she already suspected what her brother was about to say.

"Watch your back," Dimitri told her. "We're not sure if he's alone or not, and even if he is, he seems fairly resourceful. He's obviously been thinking about this for a while, so he's ahead of us in everything. Stay sharp."

She nodded. "We got this," she assured him. Then she cut her gaze over at Ezra, giving him a reassuring nod before turning back toward the door.

However, as soon as she turned the doorknob, the door was yanked out of her hand as Eve and Arlin walked in, carrying Adira between them.

"Adira!" Lainie shouted, and everyone's attention jerked toward them.

"What happened?" Dimitri asked as he left his spot, rushing to his mate's side. "Is she all right?"

"I'm fine," Adira said with a groan. "Just a little woozy, that's all."

"What happened?" Dimitri asked again as he slid his arm around her waist, taking her from the others.

As he helped her over to one of the chairs, Adira filled them all in on what happened at her place, one hand going to her head as she did. As she spoke, Dimitri examined the blood coming from the top of her head, moving his fingers through her hair as he peered at her scalp.

The doc finished stitching Josh and then moved over to where Adira sat, telling Dimitri to get out of his way. "I really need to get a waiting room."

Adira finished telling them what she remembered about the attack, which wasn't much, as Doc cleaned her up.

"She's pretty bruised up, but she'll be all right," Doc said as leaned back. "The magic of the mate bond gave her some of Dimitri's quick healing, which is probably why she's not as bad as she looks."

Adira glanced over at Ezra, her lips downturned as she stared at him. "He took Winnie," she said, and Ezra felt the knot twist in his gut, fear for Winnie filling him. There was no telling what Mattox would do to her now. If he saw her with Adira, he would assume Winnie betrayed him. "It was the first thing I saw as I woke up. He slapped her across the face, knocking her out, and then threw her over his shoulder and took off out the front door. I tried to go after them, but I was still too weak." She chuckled slightly, shrugging. "I did make it to the front porch, at least, before falling down again."

"That's when I walked by and saw her," Eve said, taking over the narrative. "I called Arlin, and we brought her here. I never saw the gorilla with Winnie, however."

"I'm sorry you two got hurt," Ezra said, bouncing his gaze

back and forth between Adira and Josh, before settling it on Dimitri. "I need to find him. I can't let Winnie get hurt, as well."

"We'll find her," Dimitri promised as he stood up from where he squatted next to Adira. "But we need to do this smartly. He's way ahead of us, as I said, and I don't want anyone else in his crosshairs." He turned back to Ezra. "But, I promise, we'll find her."

Ezra gave the alpha a curt nod but said nothing. He knew these people would do what they claimed, but he couldn't allow them to get themselves hurt because of something out of his past. This was something he needed to do on his own.

Glancing once more at Josh, he forced a smile onto his face and then told them he wanted to look around, promising not to do anything stupid. He lied, of course. He had every intention of doing something stupid. What had Winnie's reading last night told him? To trust his gut. And right now, his gut told him he needed to do this alone.

He stepped out of the doctor's office and into the humid Florida air. It made sense that he was the one to go after Mattox by himself. Mattox didn't want to kill him, just everyone else around him, the people he cared about. Ezra refused to allow that to happen. These people meant the world to him, and he would sacrifice anything to protect them. Just like he would for Winnie.

He turned, heading for the woods. Mattox would be at the abandoned airport; he was sure of it. Mattox wasn't the type to camp in the woods, nor did Ezra see the other man staying in the rickety motel up the road. That basically left the warehouse, which would allow him to come and go undetected and give him plenty of room to work out his plan to destroy Bull Creek. Now, all Ezra had to do was find the man. It shouldn't be too hard. Just a typical needle in the haystack. He sighed as he entered the woods, keeping as much to the shadows as he could as he worked his way to the abandoned airport.

Once he reached the edge of the airport, he stood there, staring out at the empty buildings, broken-down vehicles, abandoned planes, and cracked concrete. Somewhere out there was his Winnie. He only prayed he would reach her in time. As much as he wanted to dart from out of those trees, racing down there, ripping doors off hinges until he found her, he knew there would be booby traps everywhere. That was just the way Mattox worked. Winnie would be there, but who knows what she would be surrounded by?

He sighed as he inhaled deeply, hoping to catch a scent of the man. Instead, however, he caught the scent of several other animals, which caused him to lower his head, shaking it. He should have known.

Josh stepped up beside him, wincing a little as he tripped a over a fallen branch he must not have seen. "We all knew you'd come straight here," he said, reaching up and placing a hand on his freshly stitched gunshot wound. "Knew you'd do something stupid."

Ezra sighed. "Enough people have gotten hurt over the years because of me. I'm lucky none of them have died." He glanced over at his friend. "Just a few inches to the right, and you wouldn't be here talking to me."

Josh shrugged and then immediately moaned from the pain of the movement. "That's not on you," he said. "That's on him. We can't stop being who we are, just because there are assholes out there like this Mattox fellow. And who we are is a family who helps each other, standing by them no matter what."

"He's right, you know," Dimitri said as he emerged from the woods, Alanna and Adira with him. "We are a family, and if Winnie is your mate, then that includes her. Whatever happens, we'll face it together." He stepped to the edge, glancing out at the warehouses before turning back to Ezra. "But, we need to know everything you know about this man so we can be as safe as possible. So, what do you have?"

Ezra took a deep breath, crossing his arms over his chest. "Mattox is meticulous. He's also extremely patient." He told them of the bomb incident the last time he ran into Mattox. "He's a determined individual and will go to extreme lengths to accomplish his goals. Who knows how long he waited out there to take a shot at Josh? There's no telling what we'll find when we go in there."

"And you're sure he's in there somewhere?" Alanna asked, running her gaze over the area in front of them, scrutinizing every nook and corner.

"I do," he told her. "Don't ask me how, but in my gut, I know she's here." Winnie's reading last night filled his head again. Follow your instincts. Well, his instincts told him Winnie was there. "I need to find her."

"We'll find her," Dimitri assured him. "But, as I said, we need to be careful. Lainie and Rance are prowling the end of the runway, checking out the sniper's blind first, and then they'll search the rest of the area. Eve and Arlin are coming in from the back of the warehouses, and Wes, Jake, and Noel are coming in from the road. Karena is ready if we need her, as well. Her and the vampires are waiting around the back of the property."

"I still think this place would make a great location for a Halloween party," Josh said.

Alanna shook her head. "Will you stop with your parties?" She glanced over at Dimitri. "What do you want us to do?"

Dimitri sighed. "The only thing we can do. Go slow and easy, keep an eye on each other's backs, and watch out for those booby traps Ezra mentioned." He glanced around at the others. "Just be careful."

Ezra nodded, glad that his friends were there to help him, but wishing they were tucked safely away in their cabins, as well. He watched as Alanna and Josh walked off to his right, and Dimitri and Adira went to the left. He stood there for a moment, watching his friends as they made their way to the ground below, knowing that each one of them put their lives in jeopardy to help him.

He sighed as he started down to the airport below. *I'm coming, Winnie. Hold on.*

Chapter Nineteen

She sat in the chair, her arms tied tightly behind her, as she stared at the warehouse doors in front of her. She knew what Mattox intended. She watched as he set the bomb in place, two bombs actually, one in the back of the warehouse and one in the front. No matter which way Ezra or his friends came in to find her, Mattox's bombs would get them, and her in the process. And she didn't doubt that Ezra's friends would be with him. They seemed the type never to give up or to turn their backs on people, especially friends. She had waited her whole life to have a group of people around her like that, people who were loyal, sacrificial, trusting. Loving.

As soon as Mattox set the bombs, he walked over to her,

sneering. "You'll die as soon as someone enters those doors, and I hope it's not Ezra who does. I want him to watch you burn, knowing he's the reason for it. Then he'll know my pain."

"Your pain?" she scoffed, shaking her head. She was scared, her body trembling as she sat there, but she still couldn't believe the delusional audacity of the man in front of her. "You left your brother there to die, remember? You didn't even try to help him. I was there. Your driver wanted to go back, but you forced him to drive away, leaving your brother there to die. I highly doubt you feel any pain. Just humiliation that they bested you and revealed the coward you truly are."

"Coward?" he said, a sinister snicker twisting his lips. "Cowards don't achieve what I have."

"Please," she said, sighing. "Cowards fight with bombs. Cowards attack little kids and women. Cowards run while their brothers face the law. You're one of the biggest cowards I know. You won't face Ezra head on because you know he'll kick your ass."

Mattox stood there glaring at her, his lips turned up into a snarl.

Winnie arched an eyebrow as she glared back at him. The fact that he said nothing told her that he knew she was right. Ezra would kick his ass, and she couldn't wait to see it happen.

Then he lifted his head, taking a deep breath in through his nose as he closed his eyes. Grinning, he dropped his gaze back to her. "Seems your hero has arrived. I can smell his scent on the wind. I think I'll leave you to enjoy your reunion, brief though it will be." He shook his head. "Sad. We could have accomplished so much with your power and my connections."

"I never wanted to work with you," she told him. "This is the better option. I just wish I would have taken it sooner."

He shook his head, and then she watched as he shifted, his

gorilla ripping from him as his bones popped and snapped, dark fur slipping out from under his flesh, his whole body transforming as he roared up at the ceiling. She couldn't imagine going through that every time. Just watching it was painful enough.

While he shifted, she tried to wiggle herself out of her bonds, reaching down with her magic to try and coerce the ropes to twist loose. With a deep breath, she reached out to the elements surrounding her, calling them to her. Dirt filled the crevices of the warehouse, water from past storms still formed puddles along the edges of the building and on its roof; she pulled from the air around her, taking everything she could from the resources that surrounded her and pulling them into her core. She was not the weakling he assumed she was, and he would regret underestimating her before it was over.

Once his shift finished, he stood in front of her, blowing out a huge huff of air from his nose before he turned, lumbering over to the edge of the warehouse. She watched as he gripped the metal support and scrambled up to the ceiling, swinging himself over to one of the skylights at the top, and out onto the roof. He was gone, and she couldn't be happier. At least she didn't have to listen to him blabber on anymore.

Relaxing her muscles, she took a deep breath, reaching out for her magic. It was time to get these damn ropes off. Then she would work on the bombs. If she could set the explosives off while Mattox was still on the roof, she could take him out with her. She just prayed no one else was near enough to get caught up in the blast. It was the only way to keep Ezra and his friends safe. She owed him that much.

~ ~ ~ ~ ~

Ezra stepped onto the concrete, turning his head in every direction as he searched for Mattox. He could see the others, each pair scanning their surroundings. Eve and Arlin's tigers prowled along the front, their movements slow and methodical. Dimitri's panther paced beside Adira, and Ezra could see the blue sparks of her magic crackling around her fingertips. Out on the runway, he watched as Rance's wolf sniffed the ground and Lainie searched the nearby bush. Wes, Jake, and Noel checked each warehouse one at a time, Jake in his bear form, sniffing along the edges for explosives. Ezra had made sure they knew Mattox didn't fight fair, warning them to watch each step for tripwires and booby traps. It relieved him that they heeded his warnings and took things slowly, even though everything in him screamed to hurry up and find Winnie.

He scanned the rooftops of the warehouses, holding his hand over his eyes to block out the sun. There was no way he had gotten this wrong. Mattox had to be there. He just needed to find the bastard.

He turned down an alley between two of the buildings, reaching out with his senses for anything that might tell him know which way to go. As he neared the end of the buildings, a large explosion ripped the silence, sending flames and smoke into the air, the force powerful enough it slammed Ezra into the side of the building. He rolled to the side, pressing his back against the metal wall as he caught his breath, shaking his head from where the ringing filled his ears.

Winnie! Fear filled him as an icy grip clutched his heart. Shoving himself off the wall, he sprinted toward the explosion, praying no one had been caught in the blast.

He rounded the corner and saw Eve's tiger sprawled on the ground, but moving as Arlin reached her, pressing his forehead to hers. Adira ran toward the explosion, Dimitri's panther beside her, and from the other direction ran two wolves, Josh, and Lainie.. He had no idea where the triad was, and anxiety gripped him in its paralyzing grasp that they had been closer to the blast.

He jerked his attention to the destruction, one end of a warehouse crumbled in on itself as metal bent in all directions, most of it scattered along the concrete. Flames filled the air with smoke, burning what it couldn't melt, and the ceiling dangled in on itself like a broken limb that refused to let go and fall to the ground. Ezra peered through the gaping wound at the front of the warehouse, trying to see if anyone had been inside, but all he could see was smoke billowing in all directions, snagged by the wind, and blanketing the interior.

"Winnie!" he cried out as he raced closer to the rubble.

Be careful, Dimitri called out to him as they reached the warehouse. *There could be more bombs.*

A roar ripped the air as parts of the ceiling flew in all directions. When Ezra jerked his attention upward, he saw Mattox's gorilla shoving debris off his body and hurling it to the ground below. *That son of a bitch survived the explosion.* Then Ezra felt his brows furrow as he stared back at the inside of the building. If he was up there, he wouldn't have set off the bomb, so who did?

Oh, my god! Winnie! He turned, sprinting toward the burning warehouse, but before he was halfway there Mattox screamed out his name, bringing him to a halt as he turned his gaze back to the roof.

Your precious witch gave her life for yours, Mattox sent as he hurled another chunk of metal to the side. *You're always getting people to do your dirty shit. Hell, look around you. You're surrounded by people willing to get themselves killed for you. And you're selfish enough to let them.*

Ezra glared up at the gorilla, anger coursing through his body. There was no way he was right, no way Winnie could be dead. "I don't need them to take you down," Ezra yelled up at the gorilla.

"I'm more than capable of doing that on my own. Why don't you come on down and find out?"

He saw Dimitri, now in his human form, glance over at him, and Ezra motioned to the alpha to check inside the warehouse. Dimitri gave a curt nod as he turned to Josh, Adira already on her way over to the wounded Eve.

Ezra turned his attention back to Mattox, trusting his friends to find and take care of Winnie. He just needed to buy them time. Besides, this was between him and Mattox.

Slowly, he walked away from the burning warehouse, drawing Mattox's attention to him and off the others. "What's the matter, Mattox? Chicken shit? I heard how you just sat there and watched as we took your brother down. You didn't even have the balls to come back and help him." He kept walking toward the next building, keeping his gaze on Mattox who turned with him as he walked, keeping Ezra in his line of sight. "Come on, you little monkey. Fight like a big boy."

As he reached the other warehouse, he turned, walking backward so he could keep his gaze on Mattox. Smirking, he lifted his arm and made a come hither gesture with his hand. Out of the corner of his eye, he watched as Rance and Alanna made their way into the destroyed building.

Mattox roared as he leaped from one roof to another. *I'm going to enjoy killing you.*

"You'll kind of need to come down here to do it," Ezra said, shrugging. "I don't think you've got it in you, though, which is why you're still up there." Once he reached the far end of the warehouse, completely out of sight of the others, he stopped, hands on his hips. "Now, why don't you come down here so I can snap that neck of yours." And then he shifted, his body transforming into that of his bear, dropping to all fours as his body stretched in some parts and shrunk in others until his bear bellowed up into the sky.

Mattox roared as he raced to the edge of the building, dropped over the edge and grabbed the gutter. Swinging slightly, he pressed, his feet to the side of the building and shoved off, falling to the ground below as he reached for Ezra, his arms outstretched.

Ezra's bear went up on his hind legs, growling as he braced for Mattox. The gorilla's momentum kept him barreling toward Ezra, and as soon as he was within range, Ezra grabbed the gorilla's arms, spinning, and hurling the beast away from him.

Mattox kept flying through the air, roaring as he flailed his arms and legs in a vain attempt to stop.

Ezra dropped to all fours, darting across the concrete toward the gorilla, who finally hit the ground, skidding several feet before he managed to get his legs under him. By the time Mattox was back on his feet, Ezra leaped into the air, catching the gorilla in the midsection and flying backward again, the two of them hitting the ground and rolling over and over.

Mattox rolled to the side, lashing out with his fist, and catching Ezra on the jaw. Pain ripped through Ezra's head, splotches of white light exploding behind his eyes as he fell back to the ground, his head hitting the concrete hard. He could feel the cuts and gashes gouging into his flesh.

You won't beat me, Mattox roared. *You're going to die today, just like that witch who betrayed me.*

Ezra rolled back over onto his paws, a low growl ripping from him as he curled his lips away from his teeth. He stepped to the side, circling Mattox as he searched for a way past the man's defenses. There was no way Mattox walked away from there today. *Do you realize how much you talk?*

Mattox stepped closer, and Ezra stood on his hind legs, his arms out. *Don't worry. You won't have to hear my voice much longer. You'll be dead.*

Ezra growled and lunged, only instead of going straight for Mattox, which is what the gorilla expected, he dodged to the left. Mattox rushed to meet his movement, not catching Ezra's change of direction in time. Ezra swung his paw, clotheslining the other animal across the neck, knocking him off his feet and backward to the ground. Ezra dropped to his paws, landing on the gorilla's chest with all his might.

Mattox howled, reaching up to grab at the bear, but Ezra raked the gorilla's chest with his claws, leaving deep red gashes as blood poured out. He then swiped at Mattox's face, knocking his head back to the ground, a loud crack ringing out as he hit the concrete. Ezra backhanded the man, and then hit him again. And again.

Blood sprayed from Mattox's mouth and nose, his eyes clenched as he grew weaker and weaker, his arms rising in his attempt to drag Ezra off him but falling short. Finally, he just collapsed, unconscious.

Ezra stood there, towering over the gorilla as he screamed his frustration down at the man, angry that the fight was over already. The gorilla laid there, alive, but knocked completely out.

Satisfied that Mattox wasn't moving anytime soon, Ezra stepped away, turning toward the burning warehouse. He only took two steps before he saw Wes and Dimitri stepping out of the building, Winnie's body in their arms, unmoving.

Ezra lifted his head to the sky and roared.

Chapter Twenty

"You know I can sense you out there, right?" Winnie winced as she tried to lift herself up, moving further up in the bed until she felt the wall behind her for support. Ezra's constant mothering would be the death of her before it was over.

Ezra poked his head around the corner, a sheepish smile on his face. "Sorry," he said. "I heard you stirring and wanted to make sure you were all right. That's all."

She chuckled softly as she motioned him into the room. "I'm fine. Just sore as hell."

He stepped into the bedroom, still naked from where they had woken up that morning, and moved over to sit on the side of the bed next to her. He placed a hand on her stomach, as he gave her that concerned look of his, one she grew used to seeing since she woke up in Doc Henderson's office two days ago.

She hadn't remembered much once she made up her mind about setting off the bombs. She had moved toward the back of the warehouse and then used her power to set off the explosive device on the other end of the building by the front doors. As soon as it went off, the force knocked her backward, and she hit her head on the back wall. All she remembered after that was the ceiling caving in on her before she blacked out, assuming she was dying.

"You know, if I had bit you the other night while we were…" Ezra motioned to the bed, his brows raised. "Then you'd have some of my healing powers and probably be back on your feet again by now."

She laughed, as she leaned her head back on the pillows. "Hindsight is great, isn't it?"

He laughed with her, nodding. "Don't worry," he told her, leaning forward and kissing her softly. As he leaned back, he smiled down at her. "As soon as Doc gives you the thumbs up, I intend on taking care of that little mistake."

"Oh, do you now?" she asked, one brow cocked. "And don't I get a say in this?"

He leaned back, concern etched on his face. "I thought you wanted… I mean, did I misread..?" He sighed, his shoulders slumped as he frowned. "I'm sorry. I just thought the other night meant you felt the same way I did."

She reached out, taking his hand in hers and pulling him closer. "Wipe that frown from your face," she told him. "I love you. Never doubt it. I want it, as well. Your mark on my shoulder. That special bond. You in my life forever."

His frown turned around, his eyes lighting up.

She patted the bed beside her, and Ezra shifted so that he laid down beside her, his head on her pillow as he slid his arm around her shoulders so she could lay her head on his chest, her breasts pressed against his side. "Forever sounds good to me," he told her. "I've been waiting for a forever."

"Well, I'm glad I finally arrived," she told him, nuzzling down deeper into his embrace. Closing her eyes, she sighed, breathing in his scent. "I'm lucky to have you in my life."

"I'm the lucky one," he told her, squeezing her tighter. "I'm also glad this mess is over with, and we can start our life together."

She nodded, her head sliding along his chest. "Me, too."

Kacey and Liam from Para-Force showed up Sunday, taking Deran and Mattox into custody. They assured them the spell Winnie had put on Deran would last until Millificent decided to remove it. They also had special handcuffs to keep Mattox from shifting, making him safer to transport. They only stayed long enough to have a quick drink with Ezra at the cabin, making sure he was all right before they took off once more. There were other criminals out there to catch, after all.

As soon as the Doc finished mending her, Ezra took her straight to his cabin and slid her into his bed. He had curled up beside her, cradling her until she was fully awake and ready for food, her head splitting from where she hit it on the metal wall. Eve had healed quicker, her wound slight from a piece of flying shrapnel. The others had some scrapes and bruises, but that was it. Winnie took the brunt of everything, just as she had planned.

Of course, Ezra scolded her severely for taking such a risk with her own life, assuring her that he would have found her. But him getting hurt wasn't a risk she had been willing to take.

She slid her hand down his stomach to his cock, stroking it slowly. "Of course, I think I'm lucky in several other ways, too."

A low groan rumbled out of his mouth as she felt his body

stiffen under her. "You're supposed to be resting," he told her. "If you keep that up, you won't be resting."

She leaned up, grinning at him. "And who said I want to rest? I can think of better things to do while we're here in bed." She leaned back down, kissing his chest. "Besides, didn't you say something about the mate bond giving me some extra healing mojo?"

"Yes, but..." He sucked in another breath. "You're still sore from the explosion."

She continued to jack him off, her hand sliding up and down on his hardness as she planted soft kisses over his flesh. "Then be gentle," she told him in between kisses. "But I want you. Now." She slid down his chest until her lips hovered above the head of his cock and then lapped at the pre-cum at the tip.

His groans filled her ears as she felt him rest his hand on top of her head. She swallowed his manhood, sucking on him as she continued to stroke him. His hips thrust slightly, driving into her mouth as she swirled her tongue around his pulsing shaft, tasting him and savoring the feel of him in her mouth. This was the best medicine, being there with him like this. She couldn't wait to feel him inside of her once more. She burned with the need of it.

~ ~ ~ ~ ~

Ezra groaned louder, his hand on her head as she bobbed up and down on his shaft. He couldn't believe she was wanting this with as sore as she had to be after what happened. Still, there was no way he would stop it, either. He wanted it just as badly.

She slid her mouth from his cock, licking her lips as she glanced up at him. She bounced her brows as she grinned over at him. "I want you," she told him, and he felt his pulse race as his bear roared with a hunger he hadn't felt before.

He grabbed her as he slid around onto his knees, spinning her so that she was on her hands and knees, facing away from him.

"Trust me," he said. "I want you, as well, but are you sure? Once I do this, there's no taking it back."

She glanced over her shoulder at him, and he could see the passion burning in her eyes. "I won't take it back," she assured him. "I want to be your mate."

He slid behind her, his throbbing cock aimed straight at her wetness as he positioned himself behind her, one hand on her ass as he guided his cock to her slit. He stared down at her perfect ass as he shoved his cock into her, her pussy swallowing him as she cried out. God, he hoped he wasn't hurting her. But, then again, she asked for it, and he loved giving her what she wanted. He loved being buried inside of her, as well. He eased back out of her only to thrust into her wetness one more time, picking up the pace..

Winnie clutched the sheets, gripping them tightly as she shoved herself back onto him. "Yes!" she cried out. "God, yes."

He continued to pound into her, the sounds of their sex bouncing off the walls. It didn't take long for him to feel his orgasm building, ready to shoot into her. Scooping her up under her breasts, he lifted her, pulling her up so that her back pressed against his chest. Sliding a hand to one of her breasts, he pinched at her nipple as he leaned down close to her ear. "I hope you're ready for this," he whispered, just as he felt his climax hit, his cum filling her. His teeth shifted as he opened his mouth, and he clamped down on her shoulder, sinking his fangs into her flesh.

Winnie cried out, and then her body started to shake as she gripped his leg, digging her fingernails into his flesh. "I'm coming!" she screamed out as he finished filling her with his passion, her body thrashing against him.

He held her until her body stopped shuddering, her breathing sliding to ragged pants as she loosened her grip on his thigh.

"Oh, god," she whimpered, dropping her head back to chest.

"That was… Oh, god, that was amazing. I felt it. Felt the magic of the bond as you bit me."

He lowered her to the bed once again, sliding in behind her until he could wrap his arms around her and pull her tightly against him. "I love you," he told her. "And I need you in my life."

He felt her grip the arm of his that wrapped around her, squeezing it. "I will always be in your life. I have no plans of going anywhere. Ever."

He nuzzled into her neck, kissing her. "It feels as if my life just started."

He felt her nod, her head sliding against his chest. "I know what you mean," she told him. "We both have a past to forget, and a future to live for now. I want that future with you."

"This is the fortune I needed," he told her. "Right here in my arms. The something deeper. This is all I need."

She kissed his arm as she settled back against him, and he felt everything in his life had led him right to this moment. This was the place; this was the time. Their time, and he intended to make the most of it.

About the Author

Author of the popular series, *Destined Mates*, Robbie Cox started writing to escape—escape his teachers, escape his fears, even to escape his insecurities and doubts. However, his stories of seduction and adventure, not only allowed him to hide in the lives of his characters, but also captivated those who wanted to escape with him. Now, he enjoys a full-time career as a storyteller and novelist, creating rich worlds of fantasy adventure, paranormal action, and steamy romance. He invites readers to run away with him - to escape, getting lost in the seduction of adventure.

When not writing, Robbie is often found on his back porch enjoying a cigar, a scotch, and a good story. He derives pleasure from his large family and his crazy group of friends who provide the inspiration for his blog, *The Mess that Is Me*.

His series include, *Destined Mates*, *The Warrior of the Way*, *The Cauldron Coven*, *The Witches of Savannah*, and *The Bull Creek Chronicles*.

Connect with Robbie online:

Website ~ www.robbiecox.net
Facebook ~ https://www.facebook.com/robbiecoxauthor
Twitter ~ http://twitter.com/CoxRobbie
Pinterest ~ http://pinterest.com/robbiecoxauthor
Goodreads ~ http://www.goodreads.com/RobbieCox
Instagram ~ http://instagram.com/robbiecoxauthor
Bookbub ~ https://www.bookbub.com/authors/robbie-cox

For up-to-date news on Robbie's latest releases, book signing events in your area, and giveaways, follow Robbie's newsletter - www.robbiecox.com

You can also join Robbie's reading group, Robbie's Rascals, for more updates, extra giveaways, and even more fan involvement - http://bit.ly/1LdzaL

Other Books by Robbie Cox

Warrior of the Way
Reaping the Harvest
Lore Master
The Warrior's Blade
Summerlands

The Cauldron Coven
Death's Shroud
Daughters of Darkness
Chaos Magicians

Halloween Seduction
Come Halloween
Behind the Mask
Halloween Seduction

The Witches of Savannah
Enter the Witch

The Bull Creek Chronicles
Alpha Rising
Panther Hunted
Bear Necessities

Destined Mates
Magic's Mate
Mate's Appeal
Mate's Touch
My Lover's Mate
My Mate's Wife

Visit www.robbiecox.net to find out more about these great books by Robbie Cox!

Also writing as R.C. Wynne